Ransomed for the Sheikh

A NOVEL BY

Annabelle Winters

Books by Annabelle Winters

The CURVES FOR SHEIKHS Series

RANSOMED FOR THE SHEIKH

A NOVEL BY

ANNABELLE WINTERS

2018
RAINSHINE BOOKS
USA

Copyright Notice

Ransomed for the Sheikh

1

Madeline Morris spat blood. It didn't bother her. She'd been hit in the face before (you shoulda seen the other guy . . .), and this was just a busted lip. At 16 she'd already had her nose broken twice learning how to fight, and by the time she was old enough to buy cigarettes or vote, she'd come to enjoy the metallic taste of blood. It was like a magic potion that took her over the edge, gave her that last bit of fire to finish a fight her way.

"Always work a right-hander clockwise," her fighting instructor would tell her. "Keep his dominant side in check. That's it, Maddy. Stay tight, compact, elbows close to your body. Gives him a smaller target, and allows you to generate more power from your legs. You'll always be shorter than most of your opponents, but you have a strong lower body, so you'll need to get in close and finish with the uppercut. There you go. Oh, shit . . . OK, stop. Don't kill him, Maddy! We're running out of sparring partners here!"

"Tell Dad to give him an extra ten grand for the broken jaw," Maddy would mutter, spitting out her mouthguard and grinning as she watched men bigger and taller than her go down hard, their eyes going wide in shock when they got a full taste of Maddy's tight fists of feminine fury.

By twenty-five, Maddy Morris was already known on the streets and alleys of Atlanta as a top collector for her father's organization, and her record was almost perfect. The only folks who didn't cough up the cash were those that had the good fortune of being killed by someone else first—and even then, Maddy Morris and her father would go after their next of kin for the debt.

The Morris Family didn't get messed with much— mostly because they stayed within their zone: the bookie business. Charles Morris, Maddy's father, had started out as a bookie, and he'd stayed in the business, always resisting the temptation to expand into drugs, robbery, protection, or making hits for money. It kept them out of competition with the larger mafia network, the international drug gangs, and even the local street runners. If anything, their biggest competition was Vegas!

Is that who these guys are, Maddy wondered as she sucked on her broken lip and scanned the dark room where she'd been locked for the past three days. They'd ambushed her on a routine collection—well, not so routine: Maddy had sensed something was off when she got there and the guy answered the doorbell. Nobody answered the doorbell when they saw Maddy and her henchmen on the front porch.

Two shots had rung out almost simultaneously, and Maddy's guys had dropped immediately as blood splashed on the white painted walls of the small colonial-style house on the outskirts of Atlanta. She'd been startled, but she didn't run or even duck down, instinctively knowing that if she were the target, she'd already be dead. Her men had been taken out with precision, which meant that someone with serious skills had planned this. Serious skills, and serious plans.

She hadn't seen a face through all of it, and when the masked men came from all directions to take her, she'd just smiled and taken deep breaths, remembering her training and telling herself that it was a good sign they wore masks. It meant that letting her live was an option. Still, she'd tensed up when they went for her hands. Maddy never carried a gun or a knife— her fists were her weapons. And so when they tried to get those heavy-duty plastic ties around her wrists, she'd shoved off and that's when she'd been hit in the mouth. The blow had been solid, just enough to get her blood pumping. Oh, God, how she'd have loved to go one-on-one with them. Line them up and give each of them a chance to try their worth against her in the ring. Of course, they knew this, and they had her outnumbered to the point where even the taste of blood wasn't enough to make her try anything too stupid.

She didn't say a word until they got to where she was now. She'd been gagged anyway, and the black hood over her brown tresses wasn't conducive to conversation. She'd tried to follow a mental map of the twists and turns of the van she'd been pushed into, and when it stopped she vaguely knew they were on the West side of Atlanta. Then they'd tossed her into this room, and finally she'd spoken:

"I know what each one of you smells like," she'd said. "And when the time comes, I'll be able to pick up your scent in a crowded room if I have to."

The man who'd hit her turned and gave her a thumbs up, clearly not wanting her to even hear his voice. It sent a vague chill down Maddy's back, but it also gave her more confidence that they weren't going to kill her. Not yet, at least. And so if this wasn't about revenge, a vendetta, or something personal, then it had to be about money.

But this sent another chill up her spine, because although she and her father did very well, they were still just working-class gangsters. Charles Morris's decision to stay away from the big-money crime had kept them in business, but had also made sure they stayed relatively small-time. They'd never expanded beyond Atlanta. They never did more than take bets, offer the occasional street loan (only to existing clients), and then collect with a high degree of efficiency. They also paid their debts with a high degree of efficiency, Maddy reminded herself, and maybe that's why they'd been targeted: because these guys knew Charles Morris would pay up. Especially for his baby girl. His only child. He'd do anything to keep her alive, and whoever these guys were, they knew it. And they also knew that they needed to keep their identities tied down and secret, or else Charles and Maddy and every thug who was loyal to them would hunt them down and string them up on a peach tree somewhere between Atlanta and Macon.

So Maddy had stayed quiet, which wasn't hard since no one had stepped into the room with her in the three days she'd been here. The door would open and someone would shove some snacks and bottled water in there. There was a commode behind a wooden partition in the far corner. No windows. No furniture.

Then on the fourth day the door swung wide open and stayed open. Immediately Maddy jumped to her feet, already in her fighting stance as she blinked in the light pouring in through the door. A man was in the doorway. Tall, broad, heavy with muscle. He smelled different—not like the guys who'd taken her. He smelled clean, exotic, rich. Like sandalwood and desert sage, red spice and tobacco leaf. He wasn't from around here, she could tell. But he was here for her. She could tell that too.

"If you attempt to use those fists on me, I will have you blindfolded and gagged, with your wrists bound to your ankles. Then my men will drag you all the way up the stairs, down the concrete driveway, and toss you in the trunk of my limousine. When we get to my private plane, you will be put in a cage in the baggage compartment, in the place reserved for transporting animals," the man said, his voice smooth and deep, with an accent that sounded Middle Eastern and re-fined, like this man was well travelled, like he'd spent time in England and Europe as well as the United States in addition to the East. But it wasn't the accent or even the words he used that got to her. It was the way he dropped those words out there. He was dead serious—so serious that he spoke with a lazy confidence that made Maddy's body tingle from the inside out. "The other alternative is you can behave yourself and walk out this door, shower and change in a hotel room, and then join me in the front cabin of my plane. I highly suggest the second alternative, because it will be a long flight, Miss Morris."

Maddy stayed in her stance, fists clenched, tongue neatly tucked away against the roof of her mouth so she wouldn't bite it off if she took a shot to the jaw. A part of her wanted to relax and listen to this man's smooth, confident voice. A part of her yearned to take that shower, to smell nice, to smell like a woman again. But she wasn't going to simply give in to some strange man with a fancy accent. She wasn't going to give in to anyone, anytime, anywhere. She had no idea what was happening other than she'd been kidnapped and tossed into this hole. This man— whoever he was—wasn't her friend. Perhaps he was the ringleader, the guy behind it all. Either way, she wasn't giving in. No way in hell.

And so Maddy stepped forward, fists tight, elbows close to her body, leading with her left as she readied her right hand to deliver the knockout punch. But the man sidestepped her with the grace of a dancer, spinning around and grabbing her from behind so fast it took her breath away. His right arm slid around her neck in a deadlocked chokehold, and he pulled her so tight against his body that she didn't have enough space or leverage to fight him off. With barely a grunt he lifted her clean off her feet, his left arm holding her by the waist so he wouldn't break her neck with his strength, and Maddy gasped when she felt the entire length of the man's rock-hard body pressed against her from behind. She could feel his massive pectorals press against her back, his hips and crotch against her round, tight buttocks, and she wasn't sure if it was the chokehold or the lack of food that was making her lightheaded, but in that moment she wanted to simply collapse against him. Still Maddy fought to stay in the fight, and she tried to elbow him, her eyes going wide when she realized it was like elbowing a stone wall, his abdomen was so hard and muscled.

"I'll kill you," she spat, gasping as she felt him slowly increase the pressure on her throat as he dragged her to the door.

"Perhaps. But not today," he whispered against her cheek from behind as she felt herself slowly being overcome by his strength. She felt him turn his head toward the door and speak to someone else: "*Iihdar-iha*," he said, and it sounded like Arabic, though she couldn't be sure. "*Mithlama qult.*"

And then he released her as abruptly as he'd overpowered her, holding her just long enough so she wouldn't drop hard to the floor. Before she could try to swing at him again, four men were on her with nylon ropes, pushing her down and twisting her body, tying her wrists to her ankles just like he'd threatened as Maddy howled in rage, snapping her teeth like a beast as she tried to fight.

Then she felt the silk blindfold go over her eyes, the gag go over her mouth, and as she breathed heavy through her nose, she felt herself being dragged up the stairs like a hog-tied animal, just as he'd said.

And just before she heard the door of the trunk slam shut above her, she heard his voice once more, his lazy confidence sending that same tingle through her bruised body:

"Now you have learned that I do not make idle threats, Madeline Morris," came his voice from above, and Maddy swore she could hear a tinge of amusement in it, perhaps anticipation. "In time you will learn more about me. More than you ever want to know. But there is no hurry. We have plenty of time. The rest of our lives, in fact."

2

THREE DAYS EARLIER

Sheikh Imraan Al-Wahaadi blinked as he tried to push away the memories brought on by the voice on the phone. Memories that brought with them the unbridled rage of a young child watching his family being ripped apart, his parents at one another's throats, his safe, secure world shattered by events he couldn't understand. And all of it traced back to an American man, a one-time friend and associate of his father's. A man called Morris.

"My parents are dead, and if I had my way, you would be too, Morris," Imraan said over the phone, breathing deep as he tried to come to terms with how the old American gangster could still be alive. He must be a fossil by now, the Sheikh thought. *Perhaps he has called to apologize, to make peace with his enemies before he moves on to the next world. Ya Allah, I should have had him killed when I had the chance. I still do not understand why I did not!*

"Imraan," came the voice of the old American.

"You will address me as Sheikh," Imraan said quietly. "We are not on a first-name basis, old man."

"Two decades ago we were," said Morris, a little strength returning to his voice. "When you were barely ten years old. I taught you to box, to deliver a punch. More importantly, I taught you to take a punch and stay upright."

The Sheikh laughed, but it was a hollow sound that emerged from his tight chest and flexed abdomen. "And you certainly delivered a punch, did you not?"

Morris was silent for a moment on the other end of the line. "And you are still standing, aren't you?" he replied after the pause. "And so is the kingdom of Wahaad. What was it . . . nine billion in oil revenues just last year? Not to mention the seven billion in fees for the solar power you've been exporting to the smaller kingdoms of the Middle East through the infrastructure you've invested in over the past decade."

"So you learned to read the *Financial Times*, old man. Congratulations. Not bad for a man who dropped out of American public school at age fourteen."

Morris laughed, the sound coming through like

a cough over the phone. "So you do remember me well enough."

"A king does not forget his enemies, Morris. Just because I have risen above the act of revenge does not mean I have forgotten."

"Fair enough," Morris said. "You were too young to understand what happened back then. And so I won't blame you for holding on to it for all these years."

Imraan ignored the concession—or perhaps it was a provocation. Either way, he wasn't taking the bait. "What do you want, Morris?" the Sheikh asked quietly.

Morris was quiet, but the Sheikh could hear him breathe. "I need a loan," the old man finally said, his voice shaking as he said the words.

The Sheikh frowned, and then he burst out laughing. "The big-time American loan-shark needs a loan from a filthy Arab?" he shouted. "Ya Allah, I suspected you were going senile in your old age, but now I am certain of it."

"Imraan," came the old man's voice, a dead monotone tinged with dread. "I mean Sheikh Imraan. Listen to me. Think back to when our paths crossed twenty years ago, when you just a boy and all of us were like family. Your father, your mother, you, and—"

"Do not dare speak of my family as if you were a part of it," snarled the Sheikh. "Or else I will do what I swore to do when I was that angry boy of twelve. I swear it, Morris. Do not push me. You do not know what I am capable of, what I am willing to do . . . ya Allah, what I sometimes *yearn* to do!"

"Let me finish," Morris said. "Please, Sheikh. Let me finish."

The way Morris addressed him as Sheikh gave Imraan pause. He could sense the desperation in the old gangster's voice. And indeed, he must be desperate if he'd called Imraan after all these years. "Go on," said the Sheikh. "Finish."

"Think back," said Morris. "There was someone else all those years ago. A girl you played with in the gardens of your father's palace. A few years younger than you but almost your equal in fire and spirit even back then."

The Sheikh closed his eyes as the memories came roaring back, and his head spun as he saw images of that dark-haired girl, full of spunk, brown eyes always wide and alert, little fists always clenched as she tried to join in their boxing lessons. He'd almost forgotten her as he'd pushed the memories of that time into the far recesses of his mind. Almost. He knew the memories were there, but somehow he couldn't access them. He frowned and concentrated, and suddenly something clicked.

"Your daughter. Yes, I remember. What of her?"

"She's been taken."

Imraan paused. Then he shrugged, even though

Morris couldn't see him. "So what? You are a criminal. These are the risks of your profession."

"I know. But we've always stayed small-time, never
messed with the big outfits, never entered the world
of drug-running or stepped into old-world mafia ter-
ritory. In twenty years nobody's even tried something
like this, let alone pulled it off. It feels different. Real.
This is serious, Imraan. Sheikh, I mean."

The deferential, almost humble way Morris called
him Sheikh made Imraan pause again. The desperation was indeed real. Without asking, Imraan could
tell that Morris believed his daughter was a dead
woman if he didn't pay up. But still, Morris did well.
Certainly he was a millionaire after years of steady
work, albeit within the confines of his chosen criminal enterprise.

"You've done well enough over the years," Imraan
said. "And if I remember right, you were always careful with your money. That's what made you so good
at what you did. Have you blown it all on fancy cars
and mansions over the years, old man?"

"I can come up with twelve million in cash," said
the old man. "That is everything I have."

The Sheikh blinked when he heard the number.
Who in Allah's name would ask a small-time bookie
for more than twelve million in ransom? Were they
insane? Stupid? Or was there something else in play
here?

"And twelve million is not enough? How much do they want?"

"Forty-nine million dollars," said Morris, his voice almost breaking as if he'd lost hope.

Imraan paused and took a breath. Who the hell demands a forty-nine million dollar ransom?! If they'd targeted Morris and his daughter, surely they'd also know he couldn't pay it! Did they want to wipe him out, put him in debt to someone else? Or did they want to simply put him in a hopeless position, powerless to save his own daughter? Ya Allah, the Sheikh thought as a dark satisfaction rolled through him. It is almost something I might have come up with myself!

"Just so I am understanding you correctly," Imraan said. "You are asking me for a thirty-seven million dollar loan?"

"Yes," was the only response, the desperation heightened even in the single word. Then another word: "Please."

Imraan laughed. "Please?! Is that it? By God, both of us know you can never pay back that loan, Morris! It has taken an entire lifetime for you to squirrel away twelve million—and even that is quite impressive for a street-level bookie and loan-shark. Why in God's name would you even think about asking me for the money?"

"Because there is no one else I can ask. You know that, Imraan. Even big-time druglords and mafia outfits aren't going to be able to come up with that kind of cash in three days, let alone be willing to lend it to me! There's no one else I know who can . . . Imraan, this is Maddy. Little Maddy. You remember her. The two of you were—"

"Do not insult me by trying to play on emotions that do not exist, Morris," the Sheikh snapped, a switch flipping in him as he blocked out the few memories he had of that little girl he used to play with two decades ago. He could almost reach those memories, but it was like they were behind a wall, a wall someone else had erected. It was a sickening, strange feeling, something he'd experienced on and off for most of his life—so often that he was almost used to it. "I should hang up the phone right now and leave you and your family to your fate."

"You do that and Maddy comes back to me in a body bag, in pieces," said Morris, his voice cracking as he spoke. Any suspicion Imraan had that this was a ruse to extract cash from him was gone when he heard the hardened old gangster begin to sob into the phone. The man had broken. Imraan was his last resort. Whoever had taken her was serious, and she was dead if Imraan hung up this phone.

The Sheikh sighed as he considered his options. Thirty-seven million was a significant amount of money in absolute terms, but it was a raindrop in the ocean when it came to his net worth. He would make that much this week just from oil revenues. Add in interest, investment income, revenues from the new solar projects . . . yes, the money was meaningless. But the opportunity . . . the opportunity was priceless.

"All right, Morris. All right. Here is what I will do. I will not let your daughter die. You have my word on that," the Sheikh finally said. Then he took a breath. "But you will never see her again."

Imraan could sense the shock on the other end of the phone line. "What? What the hell does that mean?"

"The money is not a loan, because you will never be able to pay me back. The money is a fee. A bounty. A purchase price."

"A price for what?"

"For her. For Maddy Morris. I pay the ransom, and I own her."

"That's fucking insane. You can't be serious. Imraan, listen to me. I'll find a way to pay you back. I'll make a move into something else. Drugs. Hits. Whatever it takes. I'll do what I need to do. I swear it. Give me time, and I can—"

"You are not understanding me, Morris," the Sheikh said quietly as his determination solidified. "I am turning you down for the loan. This is my only offer. I pay the ransom, and I own your daughter. I give you my word I will not kill her, which is one better than what the kidnappers are offering, yes?"

There was a long pause on the other end of the phone. "Why?" came the response finally. "Why, Imraan?"

"You know why. You destroyed my family twenty years ago. And now I'm going to destroy yours. Choose, Morris. Say yes and your daughter lives, but she is my property. Say no and . . . well, perhaps you can ask Georgia Mutual Credit Union for a thirty-million dollar loan. Or simply call the FBI and tell them you are a criminal and your criminal daughter has been kidnapped by some other criminals. I am sure they will bring all available resources to bear to help you out before the deadline."

Another long silence, and then Morris answered. But this time his voice was stronger, a strange confidence in his tone, almost a manic amusement. "There's no choice, and you fucking know it," he said hoarsely. "All right. Pay those mother-fuckers, save Maddy, and she's . . . she's yours." Morris took a rasping breath over the phone, and the Sheikh wondered if the old man was chuckling. "Oh, and Imraan . . ."

The Sheikh waited for Morris to finish the sentence, but the old man did not. "And what, Morris?"

"And . . . good luck."

3

Maddy gripped the bars of the cage and pulled with all her considerable strength, but they barely rattled, let alone bent. She squinted in the dim light of the airplane's underbelly, trying to see if it was an old-fashioned padlock that she could snap open with a hairpin. Not that she had a hairpin, but perhaps she could find a nail or something on the floor.

She blinked as she felt the plane hit some turbulence, and she grabbed the bars of her cage to steady herself. The cage had been strapped to the siderails of the holding area, which seemed to be heated and pressurized. It also smelled vaguely primal, as if it really was used to transport animals. What the hell was happening? Who the hell was this guy? What the hell was that crap about "getting to know him better" and the "rest of their lives"? Was he implying that she'd be dead soon? Or that she was going to spend the rest of her life in a cage?

She took deep breaths and tried to relax. She wasn't breaking out of this cage, and there was no point using up energy trying to bend metal bars with her bare hands. She needed to save her strength for when she'd get another shot at escape, another shot at this guy who'd taken her.

For a moment Maddy thought she smelled him, the man who'd overpowered her so easily when she'd gone for him down in that basement. Yes, she'd been in there for three days and was weak and disoriented, but that was no excuse. He was quick, strong, confident. And God, he smelled nice, didn't he? Not like those first guys who'd taken her! This guy smelled clean, groomed, like he took care of himself and cared about his body.

Maddy almost laughed as she slammed her strong back against the back of the cage. She'd long since recognized that connection between adrenaline and arousal, and she knew that some of it was just her dumb body making connections that perhaps were relevant two million years ago when sex was nothing more than a man holding a woman down and taking what he wanted. She'd had sex that came close to that line before, but it had been years since a man had gotten her blood flowing like this. Maddy laughed again at the madness of where her thoughts were going in the darkness, and then she tilted her head back and screamed in the emptiness of the cargo hold. It was just to clear her head—in fact, one of her early fight instructors had told her it was a good move to scream your damn head off when you were fighting: it forced fresh oxygen into your lungs, got your adrenaline pumping, and it also had the effect of freaking the hell out of your opponent—always an advantage!

"Are you in pain or is that how you summon the flight attendant?" came his voice from the shadows, and Maddy whipped around in the darkness as his scent came to her before she even saw him emerge. "Did I hurt your delicate body when I shut down your feeble attempt to attack me? An ill-advised attempt, considering I saved your life."

"Why don't you unlock this cage and then we'll see who's delicate and feeble," Maddy snarled, gripping the bars of the cage and feeling her blood rise again. She knew she shouldn't waste energy on anger, but something about this guy's coolness got her mad. She wanted to fight him, hurt him, let herself go, let it all out.

"In time," said the man thoughtfully as he stepped into a sliver of light coming through one of the small windows of the plane's far wall. He was tall, massively broad, with shoulders that seemed to extend forever. His chest looked like two slabs of chiseled granite pushing against his fitted white shirt, and Maddy couldn't help but follow the cut of his cloth down along the masculine V of his body, past the heavy gold buckle of his leather belt, to where his linen trousers hugged his tight hips like a second skin. "You do not remember me, do you, little Maddy?"

Maddy blinked and cocked her head as she studied the man's face. It was angular, perfectly proportioned, with sharp, exotic features that were clearly Middle Eastern. High cheekbones, a bold jawline that was highlighted by contoured stubble. His olive skin was smooth and perfect, even though she could tell the man was a few years older. Did she know him? A former client? He didn't seem the type. Too well-put-together. This man didn't make bets—or if he did, he certainly didn't lose them, it seemed. No way had she ever knocked on this man's door to collect. She'd remember. And the accent made it clear he wasn't American, though there was a hint that he'd spent some time in the West.

And then the man took a step closer and she looked into his eyes. Green eyes, dark and deep like the waters of a faraway ocean. She blinked as she met his gaze, and as their eyes locked she felt a shift somewhere deep inside her swirling mind, the shift of memories sorting themselves out, old memories, buried deep, memories of a boy with green eyes and olive skin, from a time that seemed like it was another life.

Then the man blinked, and suddenly the memories were gone before they'd ever made themselves clear. Now his green eyes seemed cold, narrow, like something inside him had shifted as well, but in the other direction. A shift away from familiarity and towards oblivion, emptiness, silence. She felt a chill as she watched him slowly circle her cage, and for a moment Maddy wasn't sure which one of them was the animal. The one in the cage, or the one outside it.

He's in a cage too, came the thought out of nowhere as Maddy studied his face again. *I see it. I feel it. I smell it. Why? Who put him there? And who's going to let him out?*

A shiver passed through her as she wondered why those questions had come to her out of the blue. "Who are you?" she whispered through her bars. "And why the fuck—"

"Silence!" he snapped, those green eyes still cold, perhaps even colder now, like he hadn't wanted to reveal himself, like he was angry at himself. "I ask the questions. Do not mistake what is happening here."

"I'm in a goddamn cage on an airplane," Maddy said through gritted teeth, her blood rising to where she knew that if the cage weren't there, she'd be at his throat, ready to rip it out. "It's hard to mistake what's happening here. And even my father doesn't call me little Maddy, so that reference is . . ."

And then it came back to her in a flash of image

and splinter of sound: an older boy teasing her, calling
her a little girl as they faced off with clenched fists,
the sun beating down on them from above, the dry
desert air swirling around her bare legs, the grains
of golden sand coarse between her toes. There were
fountains in the background, the domes and towers
of a sandstone palace surrounding them. The memories were faint and fleeting, but they were associat-
ed with emotions that Maddy could sense were powerful . . . powerful enough to be denied and buried.

"You," she finally said, blinking as she tried to think
back to that time. The memories were still fleeting
and fragmented, but she could pick up hints of that
sickening feeling from back then, when her world
was turned upside down, her family ripped apart for
a reason she didn't understand. She saw an image of
a woman, an older woman, with smiling brown eyes
and an easy laugh. Maddy had seen that woman in
her mind's eye before. Her mother. But was it memory or imagination? Perhaps she'd never seen her at
all. Perhaps it was just a manufactured memory, put
together by a little girl who lost her mother at an early age and filled the void with the stories her drunk,
angry father would tell her on those hot Georgia
nights, when he'd get home with bruised fists and his
pockets full of blood-stained cash. Those were hard
days, hot days, angry days, and they were all tied together in her mind, connected to those equally hot

days under a dry desert sky, with fountains gurgling in the background, a tall, strong, green-eyed boy in the foreground.

"You," she said again, but now the memory of an older man in flowing robes washed over her, and suddenly she felt a burning hatred, almost uncontrollable, a hatred directed at everything and everyone. Somehow she knew that the man was the boy's father. And she knew that she hated him. She hated both of them.

"So you remember me," said the man, raising an eyebrow. "Very good. It cannot be very much you remember, though. Even my memories of that time are scanty, and I am older than you."

Maddy took a breath as she tried to control her breathing. "I remember . . ." she started to say, closing her eyes and gripping the bars of the cage. "I remember . . ." she said again, and then her eyes flicked open. "Your father. I remember your father, and I remember that I hate him. He destroyed my family." She blinked, almost in shock as the words came before even the memories did. "He killed my mother."

The man's green eyes widened, his handsome face almost draining of blood as Maddy said the words. Then the darkness returned to those eyes, and he shook his head, his face twisting into a deep frown.

"That is curious," he said taking a step until he was up against the metal bars of the cage, so close she could smell him again. "Because the way I remember it, it was*your* father who killed *my* mother. And now both of you are going to pay the price."

4

The Sheikh's mind felt like a whirlpool as he heard the anger in her words, saw the hatred in her eyes. She couldn't be remembering things clearly, he told himself as he fought to get some clarity on what had happened back then. But his own memories were messy, and Imraan knew enough about psychology to know that memories had their own lives, that memories twisted and turned, evolved and changed over the years.

But the emotions are real, are they not, he thought as he slowly paced around her cage, watching her turn along with him, her brown eyes narrow and focused, watching him. She barely blinked, barely breathed, her body coiled like a spring. Although she was several inches shorter than him, she was not a small woman, Imraan noted. From her stance he could see her legs were thick and muscular, her buttocks firm and round. Her curves were pronounced, and he almost smiled when he thought of what she might look like in a tight black dress, the cloth hugging her strong hourglass figure, showing off the contours of her breasts. When old man Morris called him out of the blue and this opportunity presented itself, the Sheikh had never stopped to consider what that little girl who was barely an afterthought back then might look like twenty years later. He'd never considered that she might actually be attractive.

"Good luck," Morris had told her after agreeing to trade his daughter for thirty-seven million in ransom money. "Good luck with her, Sheikh Imraan."

Yes, she is attractive, he thought as he finished his circle and stopped in front of her. He glanced at the heavy titanium combination lock dangling on the gate of her cage, and he cocked his head and looked into her eyes. Strong, attractive, with fire in her eyes and anger in her heart for something she believes happened twenty years ago. Something that could not have happened, of course. My father did not kill anyone, certainly not a woman. Of course, what I said is not quite accurate either—old man Morris did not kill my mother. She killed herself, but Morris was somehow involved. Somehow both Morris and his daughter were a part of that tragedy that ripped apart the Royal House of Wahaad two decades ago.

Imraan took several more deep breaths as he took one last circle around Maddy's cage and stopped. He rubbed his chin, flexed his shoulders, moved his neck as he felt a strange tension building in his muscles. Something about what she'd said had gotten to him, even though it couldn't be true. He had no memory of Maddy's mother—indeed, he had no idea who she was. As far as he remembered, Maddy and her father had been in Wahaad on their own, just the two of them. But then again he felt that pain at the back of his head, like the memories were locked away, pushed behind a wall that someone else had put there. Of course he knew Maddy's mother . . . he knew her better than he knew his own mother. Why couldn't he remember it all?! It was so close, so close . . . but yet . . .

"Who was your mother?" the Sheikh asked, blinking in confusion as he felt that wall in his psyche shake, knowing that just by asking the question he might be taking the bait, getting drawn into a negotiation, letting this woman get inside his head. After all, he knew nothing about her, did he? Nothing about how she'd handled herself both physically and mentally in the criminal underworld of Atlanta for the past two decades. She must be in her late twenties, not yet thirty, but she had scars on her forearms and knuckles, faint lines on her forehead and around her eyes . . . eyes that had a startling depth behind them. This was not some sheltered child of a rich American gangster. This was a woman who wasn't going to back down, who wasn't going to break—not easily, at least.

"I never knew her," Maddy replied, her eyes still locked in on his. "All I know is that she died shortly after I was born. Because of your father."

"Because of my father, or at the hands of my father?" the Sheikh said, smiling as he felt the calm return to him. "Earlier you said my father killed your mother. So which one is it? Did she die *because* of my father, or did my father actually murder her? Pick a lie and stick with it, little girl."

Maddy snorted, crashing her open palms against the cage with such force the Sheikh almost backed up in reflex. "Why don't you unlock this cage and then call me a little girl, you fucking coward?"

Imraan leaned in, his green eyes narrowed. "This cage is for your protection, not mine, little girl," he whispered. "Soon you will find that the best part of your day is when I throw you back in your cage to lick your wounds."

She blinked, and the Sheikh could see the color drain from her face for a moment. But she didn't break the eye contact, and Imraan cocked his head and swallowed hard. "That scared you, did it not?"

he whispered in that same tone. "But there is a part of you that likes fear, is there not? You recognize its power, yes? You *relish* its power, do you not?"

Maddy took a step back, blinking again. Score one for me, the Sheikh thought as he felt his jaw tighten even as he sensed a stiffening in his pants.

"And you relish your power, don't you? Though your power is only in your swollen head," she spat. "Unlock this cage, and you'll find out how little power you actually have when it's just the two of us."

Imraan's face twisted into a half-smile, and he stepped back, folding his arms over his chest and looking her up and down. She wore faded black jeans that hugged her wide hips and showed off the rounds of her ass, the contours of her thick thighs and heavy calf muscles. Her blue top was equally faded, and as she straightened her back he caught the outline of her nipples pressed against the cloth, pushing it out to where he could tell they were large and round, pert and erect. Was she aroused right now? Her round face was flush with color, her eyes locked onto his. The Sheikh knew there was a fine line between sex and violence, and he could sense that this woman had walked that line before—though he could not be sure which side of it she preferred.

"You did not answer my question," he said softly, slowing his breathing as he felt the need to take control of the pace of what was happening here. *Never fight your enemy the way she wants to fight you*, were the immortal words of Sun Tzu in the *Art of War*. That is what this woman is doing, is she not? Trying to draw you onto a battlefield where she thinks she has the advantage. Perhaps she believes you will hesitate to use force against her. Perhaps she believes she can seduce you. Perhaps she believes she can straight-up defeat you in a fight! Certainly those scars on her arms and fists show that this little girl never stopped fighting, and clearly she has won more often than she has lost. Besides, old man Morris's "clients" would certainly not be above using their fists against a woman. Had this woman taken hits before? Did she relish the pain as much as she relished the fear? Had she learned the dark art of harnessing the power of pain along with fear?

Only one way to find out, thought the Sheikh as he glanced at the titanium lock on the cage. Only one way to find out.

"Four, three, nine, six," he said, feeling a tremor go through his body, every muscle tightening and releasing even as he felt that inexplicable arousal get stronger. He could feel himself going to that dangerous place where violence and sex merged into one, that dark place which had beckoned to him in the past, was calling to him once again.

"What?" she said, frowning before following his gaze to the lock and its combination keypad. She blinked, and then she reached between the bars for the lock.

"Think very carefully before you make that choice, little girl," said the Sheikh, his eyes focused on hers as he slowly took off his heavy jeweled ring and placed it aside. "There is no one here but us. You step out of that cage, and I cannot guarantee you will be the same woman when I put you back in there."

Maddy snorted as she pressed the first number. "It's gonna be you in that cage when we're finished here," she said, a half-smile showing on her tight round face, a glint of madness flashing in her brown eyes. She glanced up at him, hitting the last three numbers in rapid succession, like she had made her choice and didn't want to second-guess herself, didn't want to give in to the fear the Sheikh could see in the depths of her eyes. "And I can guarantee that."

And then the gate sprung open and she was on him, fists flying, teeth bared, an animal through and through, wild and primal, full of fire, red with rage.

The Sheikh caught her in mid air, one hand grabbing her throat, the other slapping against her buttocks and pulling her into him to take away the momentum of her blows. He twisted her around as she gasped for air, slamming her against the wall and trying to pin her there with his body.

She hit him in the face as he did it, her knuckles getting him on the lower lip as he roared in pain. He could taste the fresh blood, metallic and warm, and he roared again as he tightened his grip on her throat. She laughed and spat at him even as she gagged, and finally the Sheikh released his chokehold just enough to let her breathe.

Then, as he felt his head spin from the blow he'd taken, as the adrenaline coursed through his veins, as this woman laughed, spat, cursed, and thrashed all at the same time, he licked the blood off his lips, smiled, and damned well kissed her. Hard, with authority, slamming his lips against hers, forcing his tongue into her mouth until she opened up and let him in, he kissed her.

By God, he kissed her.

5

She would have bitten off his tongue, but the force with which he slammed his lips against hers made her gasp and open wide for him. And then the arousal ripped through her, and before she understood what was happening she was kissing him back, spreading her legs as she felt him grind against her crotch, his heavy frame still pinning her against the wall of the plane's hold.

No, she thought. Absolutely not. And she grabbed his thick black hair from behind and yanked as hard as she could even as she tasted his blood in her mouth, the aroma somehow taking her to a place that scared her as much as it aroused her.

She pulled his hair again, and then jerked her head back and quickly forward, slamming her forehead into his nose. The man yelled in surprise and pulled back, and then Maddy went wild, hitting him in the chest and abdomen, landing uppercuts to his chin as the heavy man staggered back, raising his muscular arms in a boxer's defensive stance as she pummeled and punched.

She knew her blows to his body were having no effect. The man was all muscle, hard and lean, thick and immovable. He stayed in his defensive stance, weaving and dodging her blows as best he could, his arms coiled tight. But he didn't strike back, even though Maddy knew she was opening herself up and giving him clear shots to her face.

He can end this fight with one clean strike to my chin, she realized when she saw him almost take the shot but then clench his fist and hold back yet again. But at the same time, I can end it by bringing my knee up between his legs. Neither of us are taking that shot. Why not?

Still Maddy was punching, for a moment feeling like a little girl again, pummeling a heavy bag that barely moved from the impact of her tiny fists. She screamed as that sense of powerlessness rose up, but yet she didn't take that low shot, just like he was holding back with his fists that were the size of sledgehammers. Then she got him once more on the lip, and finally he roared and grabbed her by the hair, flipping her around and pulling her down to the rough carpet of the plane.

"Enough, little girl," he snarled in her ear from behind. "Now you will see who is in charge. Here is your first lesson."

He tightened his grip on her hair, his fingers all the way down by the roots. The pain felt good, and Maddy smiled and screamed at the same time as he pushed her down face-first, raising her bottom and smacking her hard on her rump, again and again until she felt the sting of his slaps even through her jeans and underwear. She felt him slide his fingers between her legs, rubbing her roughly as she gasped in shock at the heat rushing through her, the wetness flowing out of her almost like she'd peed herself.

"Oh, God," she whimpered, her eyes going wide as she felt him unbutton her jeans from beneath and then pull them down over her ass, spanking her so hard she knew his fingers would leave marks. "Fuck you!"

"Silence," he commanded from behind her. "You'll speak when you're spoken to, when I allow it." Then he leaned forward, pulling her head back by her hair and whispering against her cheek: "And do watch your language. I am a king, you know."

Maddy gasped as she felt his warm breath against her cheek, and she breathed deep of his masculine scent. He was so strong, so big, so in control . . . control that she knew he'd exerted by *not* striking her when he had the chance, even though she was giving him everything she had. Once more she considered sliding out from under his grasp and punching him in the balls, ending this her way, with this self-proclaimed "king" writhing on the floor. But she couldn't do it. She wouldn't do it.

Still, Maddy wasn't going to just nod her head and submit either. "America is a democracy, last time I checked, you Neanderthal. My ancestors died on a battlefield so they wouldn't have to listen to some king."

"Ah," said the man from behind, still holding her hair, his hardness pronounced against her raised bottom, those black jeans of hers still pulled halfway down her thighs, nothing but her panties separating his body from hers. "So now this is a battlefield and you are fighting for American freedom?"

"Something like that," she muttered, almost laughing. But then she gasped again as she felt his right hand slip between her buttcheeks from behind, his thick fingers running down along her crack, carefully sliding her panties down with their motion until she could feel the cool, dry air against her naked skin. Slowly he released her hair from his viselike grip, pushing her down flat on her stomach. She complied, not sure why she wasn't fighting. Perhaps it was the sudden change of pace, the unexpected lighthearted joke, the way he was caressing her smooth ass with his big hands, spreading her rear cheeks and rubbing her crack with his thumb and forefinger in a way that made her want to moan out loud.

He smacked her ass again, gently this time, then harder, three times on each cheek until she could feel her buttocks shudder and shake. She knew he was hard as a rock behind her, and her breath caught as she wondered what he was going to do, where he was going to do it, how hard, how deep, how long.

Oh, God, I'm aroused as hell, she realized, and just admitting it made a fresh wave of wetness ooze from her exposed pussy until she could feel the slickness dripping down her thighs. She was flat on her stomach, jeans down past her knees, panties down over her ass, wetness flowing between her legs. This was arousal like she hadn't experienced in years, if ever. Her fists still hurt from hammering at his rock-hard body. Her buttocks still stung from his merciless slaps. She felt herself smile again when she thought about how she'd made him bleed, how she'd chosen not to kick him in the damn balls. It made her believe that she hadn't broken, hadn't given in, hadn't submitted. It made her believe that they were even, that whatever happened now was all right, was OK, was in her control.

Her smile widened as the man pulled her jeans all

the way off, then slid her damp panties down past her ankles. Now she was naked from the waist down, exposed and vulnerable, wet and ready. She moaned as she prepared to turn, to spread her legs, to show him his prize, what he'd won by surviving one round in battle with her.

"Lesson number one," he whispered from behind her, leaning forward and pressing his weight down on her from behind even as his hand slipped between her legs, his fingers resting on the lips of her wet vagina but stopping there. "I am in control. I say when, how, why, and for how long." Then suddenly he was off her, and as she shrieked in surprise he grabbed her by the hair, pulled her to her feet, and before she knew what was happening he'd pushed her back into her cage and slammed the gate shut.

She stared at him in shock, the arousal turning to hatred so fast she almost fainted. She slammed her palms against the bars, but he'd already snapped the lock back on. She desperately punched the numbers to the combination, but the electronic lock simply beeped and flashed red.

"What the hell," she muttered, punching the numbers again, sure she was remembering them right even in her rage.

"The lock has a memory of several different combinations," the man said nonchalantly. "It cycles through the combinations. Very smart system, don't you think?"

Maddy spat at him again, reaching through the bars as she tried to grab at least her jeans if not her panties. But the man pulled the clothes out of reach, shaking his head as he smiled and folded her jeans. Then he placed her panties on top of her jeans and took a breath.

"My name is Imraan, Sheikh of the Kingdom of Wahaad," he said quietly as he tucked her jeans and panties under his arm and stood to full height.

"Whoop-dee-doo," said Maddy, gritting her teeth and sitting down, drawing her legs up into her body to cover herself. She wanted to kill him, pure and simple. She wanted him dead. "How nice for you, you goddamn freak."

The man smiled, his green eyes narrowing. He swallowed hard, his eyes closing as if he was in sudden pain. He rubbed his head, and when he opened his eyes again he looked like a different person. His eyes were unfocused, like he was in a trance. He blinked again and snapped back into focus, a look of shock passing across his handsome face, as if he'd remembered something . . . something he'd always known. "Actually it is you who are the freak, as you call it. A child of sin. The worst sin of all."

"What the hell are you talking about?" Maddy said, drawing her legs closer to her as she felt those old memories tugging at her insides.

The Sheikh rubbed his eyes, that look of shock even more pronounced on his face. He swallowed hard and smiled, but Maddy could tell he was doing his best to appear composed. Something was going on in this man's head. He was remembering things, she could tell. Things that perhaps he didn't know he knew. "Humiliation," he said quietly. "I have to destroy your father the way he destroyed my father and mother, humiliate your family the way you humiliated mine."

Maddy stared at the Sheikh. "I barely remember you at all. How could I have humiliated you when I could barely walk?"

"Your birth itself was a slap in the face to the Royal Family of Wahaad," said Imraan. "Your very existence destroyed the legitimacy of the House of Wahaad. Lowered my father's omnipotence in the eyes of his people. Brought about the suicide of my mother." He paused for a moment, his jaw tightening, those eyes narrowed to slits that shone green in the dim yellow light. "And the suicide of your own mother."

Maddy almost passed out as images and flash-backs screamed through her frazzled mind. But none of them made any sense. None of what this maniac was saying made any sense. And none of what she was feeling made any sense.

"You . . . you knew my mother?" she stammered.

The Sheikh smiled, shaking his head slowly. "The old bastard never told you any of it, did he? Never told you what he did. Never told you who you are." The smile faded, and again the Sheikh rubbed the back of his head, his eyes losing focus for a moment.

It was all Maddy could do to slowly shake her head. "No," she whispered, pulling her naked thighs so tight against her body she could barely breathe. "He just told me that something happened when we were in the Middle East on holiday. Some mix-up with local customs, and my mother was . . ."

"Your mother was what? Put to death by my father?"

Maddy blinked. "I don't . . . remember. He used to say that when I was young, when he was still drinking. But he'd always clam up when I asked him what he meant, why a Sheikh would have my mother put to death. Then when he stopped drinking, the stories stopped. He never brought it up again."

The Sheikh took a breath. "Did you ever notice that your skin tone is slightly darker than your father's?" he said after a pause. "Your features a bit sharper, your hair a bit blacker?"

Maddy glanced at her bare arms and naked legs as if she was looking at herself for the first time. "I suppose. I never even saw a photograph of my mother, so I never thought about the hair or my nose or whatever. And we're all a bit tanned down south, so I didn't really think much of that either."

"Well, perhaps you should have. Though to be fair, your mother was not particularly dark: She was half Arab, half German." He took a breath. "But she was all Wahaadi. A part of the proud Royal House of Wahaad.

A Sheikha of the Royal House, in fact." He shook his head again, his jaw twisting as he finished what he had to say. "Maddy, you are the bastard child of the second Sheikha of Wahaad, my father's second wife. A child of infidelity and betrayal. A child whose existence destroyed my family name, humiliated my father, broke my mother, the First Sheikha of Wahaad."

Maddy blinked in confusion as she stared at this green-eyed monster in front of her, his face twisted with the anger of a little boy consumed by his emotions. "So I'm your . . ." she began to say, swallowing hard. "You mean we're . . . related?"

"Not by blood," spat the Sheikh. "Just by lust, betrayal, and humiliation. And that is what will define the rest of your life, little girl. Just like it did for my father in his last days. Just like it did for me when I was a young Sheikh finding his way in the world. I thought I had forgotten it all, buried it so deep it didn't exist. But seeing you has opened something up in me, brought back memories I didn't know existed." He shook his head. "Lust. Betrayal. Humiliation. The legacy of my family." His twisted smile widened, and though his teeth were perfectly aligned and white as snow, Maddy felt a chill run through her as she stared upon the face of her captor, her owner . . . and her stepbrother. "And so welcome to the family, Maddy. Welcome to your family."

6

Sheikh Imraan watched the capital city of Wahaad expand beneath him as his private plane descended toward the perfectly straight main runway of the small airport. There were plans to expand the runways, build a new terminal, add a dozen new international flights a week. Wahaad was on the rise, an old kingdom moving into the new world. But none of it made the Sheikh happy. Not today. Today he was thinking about the girl in a cage. And that made him happy.

Ya Allah, am I a madman? A psychopath? A twisted caricature of a human being? I have my stepsister locked in a cage, stripped from the waist down like some whore, deprived of food and water for the past eighteen hours at least, if not more. And I am happy? *Happy*?

He forced a smile as he brushed aside those memories that were creating a strange restlessness behind the sickening happiness he felt. Memories of that little girl on the grounds of the Royal Palace of Wahaad. A part of him knew he was missing something, missing a part of the story, perhaps the most important part of the story. After all, Maddy must have been at least five years old in those memories. Old enough to walk. Old enough to talk. Old enough to bare her little fists and fight as they trained near the fountains of the East Wing of the Royal Palace. If everything Imraan believed were true, how could that scene fit in? How could there be memories of all of them in the Royal Banquet Hall, the old Sheikh and his two wives, each of them with their child by their side, all of them laughing and joking as smiling attendants served them steaming dishes fresh from the kitchens of the palace?

For a moment he thought of calling old man Morris and simply asking him. The old bastard was the only one alive who would know the true story, the full story, yes? After all, Imraan's father was killed in a plane crash. And both Sheikhas—Imraan's mother as well as Maddy's mother—died by their own hand: a suicide pact that was supposedly to save face but instead had broken the spirit of the Wahaadi people, broken the spirit of the young son they left behind.

But what about the daughter, the Sheikh thought as his mind drifted back to the woman in a cage. Clearly her father had told her very little, if anything about her background. And clearly there was a fight going on inside her, just like that battle raged on inside him.

A flash of pity, a splinter of remorse, a hint of guilt. But the Sheikh was an expert at brushing aside any emotions that weakened his resolve, and he closed his eyes and tightened his jaw and suddenly those thoughts were gone like smoke on a cold desert night. This was fate, and nothing was going to stop him. Not those brown eyes of hers that did something to him even though he hated to admit it. Not those curves of hers that made him hate himself for wanting her. Not that feminine scent that had invaded his senses when he pushed his face between her thighs . . . his stepsister's thighs . . . and inhaled deep of her musk.

Ya Allah, I am a monster, he thought as the plane landed with a bump that he knew would jolt the woman in the cage. But so is she. An abomination created by illegitimate lust. Yes, she is a monster just like I am. And since it is her existence, her birth, her entry into this world that twisted me into this monster, it is only right that I repay the favor by twisting her into what she truly is, was destined to be.

The Sheikh unbuckled his seatbelt and strode to the plane's holding area as the jet slowly taxied to the private terminal, where three silver Range Rovers were waiting patiently on the tarmac for the king's arrival. He'd planned to humiliate her by having her carried out in the cage, half naked like some beast he'd captured. But when he entered her presence and looked into her eyes—brown eyes that were alert and defiant, alive and unbroken—he knew he could not do it. She was his. His alone. This was between the two of them. It was no one else's goddamn business.

Satisfied at the explanation he'd given himself, telling himself he wasn't conceding to those eyes that seemed to look so deep into him, the Sheikh tossed Maddy's faded black jeans to her through the bars of the cage. Then he glanced at her underwear, crumpled and still damp, and he shook his head as he felt his cock move, his mind swirl, that strange feeling of being a monster somehow making him perversely happy.

"These I will keep," said the Sheikh, grinning as he held her black panties up.

Maddy snorted, those eyes of hers never leaving his. "I figured. You're just a sick little pervert in a muscle-bound body, aren't you? You know what, keep these too." She grabbed her jeans and tossed them back out through the bars, pulling her legs up against her body so her crotch was covered. She smiled, and the Sheikh could see the challenge in her eyes. "Now what, my sick little stepbrother? You're going to parade your sister naked through the streets of your kingdom? Show the people who you really are?"

Imraan took a breath as he stared at the panties

in his hands, her crumpled jeans on the floor. He glanced at her, feeling himself harden again when he saw her thick thighs pulled up against her body, her feet tight together, ankles perfectly covering the dark space between her legs. It was somehow both obscene and elegant at the same time, and the Sheikh had to swallow hard to hold back from ripping open that cage door and spreading those legs, pushing his face back in there, showing her that he did own her, that he was in charge.

But he held back, taking another deep breath and then smiling. "First of all, I am your big brother, little girl. And secondly, do not underestimate who I really am. I can have you strung up naked in front of the Grand Mosque and flogged if I so desire."

Maddy shrieked in laughter, bending forward, her heavy cleavage trembling as she giggled almost uncontrollably. The Sheikh could tell she was at the edge of her sanity—after all, she'd been kidnapped, starved, and almost raped over the past three days—but yet she was standing eye to eye with him in this strange battle, challenging him as he stood there with her panties in his hand while she sat on her bottom, naked and vulnerable but still in the game, still fighting, still unbroken.

"Go ahead," she whispered through her manic laughter, looking up at him from the floor of her cage. "Do it. I dare you. I fucking *dare* you!"

The Sheikh clenched his fist as a twisted rage

surged inside his hard body. He wanted to hurt her. Slap her across the face. Turn her over and spank her so hard she cried like the little girl she was. Fuck her until she screamed for mercy. But he also knew she'd won this round. He wasn't going to let anyone else see her naked. She was *his*, and somehow, someway, though perhaps she didn't even consciously realize it, this woman knew she was his and his alone.

He stood there in silence, knowing that if he turned and walked away it would mean he'd conceded, given in, been broken by her will. That wasn't going to happen.

I can cover this cage with a tarpaulin and have it carried out like she is some exotic beast of mystery, he thought as that twisted smile contorted his face once again. But a quick glance around the holding area made it clear that there wasn't anything large enough to work.

And then Imraan got it. He smiled and nodded, glancing down at the panties in his hand, the crumpled jeans on the floor. "All right, my stubborn little stepsister," he whispered, his smile growing as he picked up her jeans and slowly walked towards her cage. "If you will not dress yourself, then I will do it for you."

7

Maddy pulled her legs closer against her body as she watched the Sheikh tower above her outside the cage. He looked tall and broad, powerful and majestic, the bulge at the front of his brown silk trousers making her wet in the most sickening, beautiful way. She had very few memories of him, of that time twenty years ago—but there were memories buried in there somewhere. She could feel it. She could taste it. She could smell it.

She inhaled deep of his scent as she watched him pace around her cage slowly, like a predator waiting to pounce. But somehow she didn't feel like prey. She didn't feel like a victim. And although there was fear, it was the kind that Maddy relished somehow. Why was that? What kind of a twisted woman was she to be sitting here half-naked, aroused and wet while a man who was in total control of the situation had her in a goddamn cage?

"How's that broken lip feeling?" she asked as she heard him stop behind her outside the bars of the cage. "You ready for another round? Maybe I'll break your perfectly shaped nose this time."

"Perfectly shaped? So then you noticed," he whispered from behind, and she could hear the amusement in his voice. He was close, very close, and Maddy wanted to turn but she stayed firm, not giving in to the urge to whip around and either strike at him through the bars or crawl to the other side of the cage. "That is not the only perfectly shaped part of my body," he growled from behind her, his face so close she felt his warm breath on her bare neck. "Though you will not get the pleasure of that quite yet, little girl."

Maddy snorted, resisting the urge to jump away from him as the fear rose up in her to where she was almost wild with anticipation. God, she was a sick creature, wasn't she. Maybe she deserved to be here with this beast who said he was her stepbrother. This animal of a man who was—

And then she felt him grab her shoulders from behind, twist her around until she faced him, and as she gasped for breath she saw that he'd silently taken off his thick leather belt and looped it around the cold steel bars of her cage.

"What the fu—" she screamed as he pushed her face down and grabbed her arms through the bars, pulling her wrists together and tying that belt tight before she realized what was happening. "I'm going to—"

"You're going to do nothing but obey," he said, pulling the belt tight until she was flat on her stomach, facing the bars of the cage. "Also, you are correct. I do not want to take a punch to my perfectly shaped nose. So please sit still while I dress you."

Maddy blinked as the Sheikh stood and walked around to the front of the cage, unlocking it and stepping in. She heard him behind her, and then there was silence. Somehow she knew he was standing there and staring down at her naked bottom spread before him, and although the thought was sickening, she could feel the wetness ooze out of her and onto the cold floor of her prison. What was he going to do?

"I will give you one chance," he said quietly. "Nod your head and say you will dress yourself, and I will untie you and step outside the cage. Go ahead. All you have to do is nod your head. Give in. Submit."

She could hear the challenge in his voice, the way he'd said the last three words. "Give in." "Submit." He was responding to her dare with his own, wasn't he? He knew she wasn't going to submit. He was taunting her, playing her, forcing her to make the choice that unleashed whatever he was going to do next.

And what was he going to do next? Dress her like she was a doll? Spank her bottom and make her beg for mercy? Drop those silk trousers of his and show her that other "perfectly shaped" part of his body?

Maddy knew she wasn't thinking clearly, but she couldn't deny that the mixture of fear and arousal was making her breathe heavy, making her heart race, making her eyelids flutter. Images from two decades ago were pulling at the fringes of her swirling mind, memories that were faint but somehow tied to emotions that she knew ran deep. There was a reason this was happening, it suddenly occurred to her. She couldn't understand why, but she somehow knew she had to play this sick game through to the end. More importantly, she had to win.

She had to win.

And so when he asked her again to submit, she spat onto the floor and cursed him, called him a pervert and a psycho, kicked out her legs wildly when she felt him grab her from behind and try to pull her panties up over her rear globes. She screamed like a madwoman, realizing how insane it was that she was fighting off his attempts to put her clothes *back on*, the realization making her arousal spiral upwards to where she wanted to raise her ass and spread for him.

Still she kicked and fought, and then she felt his

palm come down on her ass, the first slap sending a vibration through her body that rattled her teeth and made her eyes roll up in her head. And then he was spanking her again, left cheek and right cheek, his heavy open palms coming down clean on the meaty part of her buttocks. The slaps rung out like gunshots as she screamed, but even through the pain she somehow understood that he was being careful to spank her just right, to make sure he was angling his slaps so he wouldn't put any pressure on her hips or get her on her tight thigh muscles where the pain would be too much. She was tied and caged, but somehow she felt safe with him, and she screamed again and raised her bum for him as he spanked her.

"There we go," he gasped from behind her, and she could hear the arousal making his voice thick, like he was choking from desire. He spanked her one last time, and then he placed his hands on her raw, stinging buttocks and massaged her carefully and slowly, his strong palms kneading her ass until she hung her head down and lay flat, exhausted, with tears streaking down her face but for some insane reason smiling.

She was smiling because his voice had brought back a memory—a memory of the two of them, a little girl crying after taking a hit from a swinging punching bag, an older boy comforting her even though he'd been the one egging her on to hit the moving bag that was way too big for her.

"We only get better and stronger if we try to do things we cannot," the boy was saying to her in that memory. "We have to reach beyond ourselves to grow. The next time you get hit by the bag, you will laugh! And the time after that you will laugh harder! Until finally you will not get hit by the bag at all because you are better, stronger, faster! You see, Maddy?"

The little girl in the dream nodded earnestly, staring up at her tall, strong stepbrother with wide eyes. And the woman on the floor of the cage widened those same eyes, tear-filled and older but still earnest, still looking to grow, to reach beyond herself.

"Why do you hate me?" she asked absentmindedly. "Why do I hate you? What happened? What happened to us, Imraan? What happened?"

She heard his heavy breathing stop for a moment, and then his hands left her body and she felt a chill go through her. Only now did it occur to her that she was naked with her stepbrother, tied to the bars of a cage, her ass stinging from being spanked like a whore. Where was all this emotion coming from? All this hate? All this . . . desire? Who were they, the two of them? Twisted, broken, warped. Were they born this way or did someone turn them into these creatures?

"I told you what happened," he replied from behind her. "*You* happened."

Maddy shook her head, unable to turn and look at

him. "But I remember us together. There are memories, Imraan. Hazy, buried, but real. I lived with you at the Palace. I know it. I must have been four or five, so what you're saying doesn't make sense." She paused and took a breath, exhaling slowly. "And if I have memories, then you do as well. Which means you know it doesn't make sense. Either you're lying to yourself, lying to me, or we're both missing part of the story. We're both missing part of what made us who we are: These angry, violent people who crave pain, relish fear, *need* it . . . I . . . I don't know what I'm saying. But I feel . . . I feel like . . . oh, God, I just don't fucking know!"

And then she was crying, her chest heaving so hard she was gasping against the floor of her cage. And suddenly he was on top of her, this stranger who was her stepbrother, her captor, her partner somehow in this twisted tale that was unfolding between them. His heavy body crushed hers like a protective blanket, and somehow she knew he was crying too, though she couldn't see or hear it. It was messed up.

So messed up.

8

"It was you who messed it up, not I," said Begum Gaurina, grimacing in the mirror as she dabbed at her blue eyeshadow and then glanced at the reflection of Begum Khalifa in the handmade oval mirror hanging in the main dressing room of their Paris penthouse apartment. "That old fart Morris was not supposed to *sell* my daughter to your twisted son like she is a piece of meat!"

Khalifa's jaw tightened as she glared back at Gaurina, the two women framed in the gold-plated mirror like it was a photograph. "It was you who turned your daughter into a piece of meat to be bought and sold the moment you agreed to this scheme, you old cunt," she replied, raising one perfectly plucked eyebrow as she spoke.

Gaurina froze, holding her brush halfway to her eyelids, her mouth hanging open for a moment. Then she burst out laughing, and Khalifa joined in, the two of them cackling like witches in the woods as they shared the long, velvet-cushioned bench and finished their makeup ritual before their weekly dinner at the restaurant *Daniel*on the banks of the River Seine. They'd lived here in secret exile almost two decades now, and they rarely left their lavish apartment for anything other than their weekly dinner out and the occasional walk through the fashion district.

Not that they showed off the latest fashions or their expensive makeup when they left the house: The two old queens were always covered in their *burkhas* and *hijabs*. Not because they were particularly bound to tradition or religion—they weren't—but because in this age of cell-phone cameras and digital facial recognition and whatnot, they couldn't take any chances of being recognized. They were dead. Anonymous. Out of sight, out of mind. That was the price they'd agreed to pay for what they'd done twenty years earlier, for what they'd done to their families, done to their children.

Their children.

9

The Sheikh watched her as she ate. He hadn't said a word after that final moment on the plane, when they'd both spontaneously broken into tears, crashing against each other in that cage.

We are both in a cage, are we not, he thought as he watched her polish off the last of the savory dishes sent by his chefs and lick her fingers as her eyes went wide with satisfaction. Eyes that had barely left him even though she was wholly focused on her food. Eyes that reminded him of something long forgotten, secrets buried, memories that a part of him knew were perhaps better left untouched.

But those parts of ourselves can no longer remained

untouched and buried, the Sheikh knew as he watched his stepsister drink her third glass of cool lemon water and then slump back against the high-backed teakwood chair and rub her belly like a child at a birthday party.

"Do you remember this room?" he said quietly, glancing up at the towering domed ceiling of the dining room of the Eastern Wing of Wahaad's Royal Palace. "This was where you and your mother lived. These rooms. Your bedroom was over there. Your mother slept in the master bedroom down the hall. Neither of those beds have been slept in for over twenty years."

Maddy blinked as she glanced at him, one hand still on her full belly. She looked beautiful, the Sheikh thought. Long brown hair, full breasts, thick thighs whose outline was prominent against the white flowing dress he'd chosen for her from his mother's old wardrobe. Then Sheikh started in his seat, swallowing hard and freezing when he realized that the memories of Maddy and her mother were suddenly there like they'd never been buried! Some of the memories, at least.

Ya Allah, he thought as he looked absentmindedly at her. What just happened? Something has opened up in me, beginning from the moment this woman came back into my life! How? Why? What?

Imraan rubbed his eyes and swallowed hard. There

was still that deep-seated sense of humiliation, that indescribably deep feeling that this woman and her father were at the root of it. But now there was a clearer memory of Maddy's mother, Begum Gaurina, the old Sheikh's second wife. Imraan could see her in his mind's eye, young and beautiful, with flowing brown hair like Maddy's. She'd always hated wearing her hijab, and would only cover her face and hair for the most solemn of public ceremonies—and even then only after long arguments with the old Sheikh.

Imraan almost choked when he realized he was aroused as those memories came rushing back. Then the guilt washed over him . . . the guilt of a young boy lusting after his stepmother, a woman who walked the halls in a see-through robe, her hair open and wild, her eyes looking into his, beckoning to him, calling him . . .

Ya Allah, no! he thought, unconsciously bending forward on his chair to hide the shame growing in his pants. It cannot be. I could not have! *She* could not have!

But when he glanced over at Maddy again the memories of her mother came roaring back so fast his head spun, his gut seized, his eyes glazed over. Yes, she'd called him into her chambers one evening, after the sun was gone, her brown hair hanging down over her breasts, her big brown nipples pert and erect beneath her white silk gown, her scent rising up to him from between her legs as the young Sheikh-to-be, a pubescent boy just discovering the pleasures of his own body, gave in to the older woman's invitation.

He remembered sucking on her nipples like a hungry pig, shuddering as she undressed him, convulsing as she took him into her mouth and made him come. He remembered the guilt mixed with pleasure when she showed him where to put himself, showed him where to touch her to get her wet, to make her moan. He remembered that filthy, choking sensation he'd felt when she turned around, bent over, raised her smooth brown buttocks, instructed him to spank her until she was red and raw, to push himself into her rear, to go as hard as he could, to pull her hair as he shot his hot seed into her anus.

Ya Allah, he thought as those memories clouded out his vision, bringing back that overwhelming sense of filth, guilt, self-loathing. What sort of twisted beast am I?

The answer came in a final memory that almost made the Sheikh pass out. A memory of one of those evenings with Begum Gaurina. An evening when she was turned face-down, bottom-up, moaning and clawing at the silk sheets. An evening where young Imraan, in the death throes of his orgasm, had caught movement out the side of his eye. As the Sheikha screamed at the force of his hard young cock ramming into her and exploding in her depths, Imraan turned towards the moving curtains and looked into a pair of big brown eyes, young and innocent, open and wide.

Little Maddy tore into the room through the curtains, screaming her head off as she battered at Imraan with her little fists, howling at him to leave her mother alone. And the Sheikha, naked and wet, simply tilted her head back and laughed at the scene. Ashamed and horrified, Imraan had pushed the little girl off him and run from the room, covering his shame as he left. Behind him he could hear Begum Gaurina's laugh, twisted and shrill, mixing with his stepsister's cries, all of it combining in a moment of such dark depth that it was all he could do to get to his private chambers before throwing up.

The young Sheikh-in-waiting did not leave his room for two days, and when he answered the knock of the outside world, it was only because of the news:

Both Sheikhas had committed suicide together. They had walked together into the Great Oasis of Wahaad, and had never walked out. They had left the old Sheikh a note explaining their reasons—a note that the Sheikh never shared with anyone. A note he claimed to have destroyed immediately after reading it twice and then having the messenger who delivered it executed.

Why are these memories coming back to me so clearly only now, the Sheikh wondered as he watched the girl at the far end of the long teakwood table where they'd once sat as a family—a family broken and twisted but still a family. I was old enough to do those things—do them willingly—and so it seems to defy reason that I could have buried those memories so deep for so long. What caused me to forget events of such magnitude for so long? Is that even medically and psychologically possible? Am I imagining things that never happened? Or am I just insane? Unhinged?

Ya Allah, I do not know. All I know is that this girl in front of me is the key. Being close to her has triggered something in me, opened up what was closed. Does she remember that night? Can I even ask her that? And if she does remember . . . ya Allah, what will she think about how my body reacts when I am with her?

That choking feeling came back to him as the Sheikh fought it, tried to push away those thoughts that he was a damaged, broken, twisted man, a man who as a boy had fucked this woman's mother and now could think of nothing else but possessing the daughter! Did he deserve to even take another breath? Were Allah's angels sighing in despair at the world that had produced a creature as sick as Sheikh Imraan?

"I don't remember," came her voice through his dark daydream.

"What?" he said, staring at her, his face burning as if with the fires of guilt.

"This room. You asked me if I remember this room,"

she said, raising an eyebrow and smiling at him. "Hello? Anyone in there? You know, you're more scary now, sitting at the dinner table with that look on your face than when you had me tied down and naked."

Her smile broke the Sheikh out of his trance, and he smiled back. "You were not scared then, and you are not scared now. Why is that, by the way?"

Maddy shook her head. "Who kidnapped me?" she asked almost nonchalantly as she picked something out of her teeth and wiped her fingers on the table-cloth like a child who'd never learned table-manners. "It was you, wasn't it?"

The Sheikh grinned. "Well, I had you in a cage, so clearly it was I who kidnapped you."

"Very funny. I mean the first set of kidnappers, my idiot brother," she said, raising her leg and resting it on the armrest of the empty chair beside hers. She wiggled her bare toes at him and raised an eyebrow, and the Sheikh felt his cock move as he glanced at the smooth curve of her naked calf. He wanted to push that white dress up over her sturdy thighs, spread her wide on that heavy teakwood chair, one leg over each armrest as he pushed his face down there and took control of her.

Careful, he told himself as he watched her dark brown eyes. She is as twisted as you are, as damaged as you are, as smart as you are, perhaps even as strong as you are. She is playing you because she sees the effect her body has on your body. She is no different from her damned mother, Imraan. Be careful. Be very careful.

Now he hated her again, hated her like he hated her mother, for what she'd done to him. And even though he knew that part of the hatred was the loathing he felt for himself, for that horny teenage boy who'd happily succumbed to the advances of his unhinged stepmother, Imraan hated her. She'd made him remember what should have stayed forgotten. She was a symbol of what was rotten in him, twisted in him, broken in him. Those eyes of hers had witnessed what should never have been witnessed, and whether she remembered it or not, those eyes were accusing him, blaming him . . . beckoning him?

Stop, he told himself, closing his eyes as he felt a dull pounding at the back of his head, like those old memories were gleefully chipping away at what was left of his sanity. He could feel the fever rise, and for a moment he was worried what he might do. But he took another deep breath, swallowed hard, and told himself he was overreacting. Perhaps things were not as twisted as they appeared. Perhaps this woman could help him find what little of him was still undamaged. Yes, perhaps, thought the Sheikh as he opened his eyes and smiled.

She'd put her foot back down on the floor, and she was sitting with her arms folded across her chest, hands hidden from view in her armpits. Those brown eyes of hers were still focused on his—indeed, she'd barely broken the powerful eye contact the entire time they'd been together—but the Sheikh sensed something different in her look. He cocked his head and frowned, his body tingling as that sense of something being off escalated to where he could feel the adrenaline start to pour into his bloodstream.

Then he saw what was different. Amongst the remains of the food was a dish of hard cheese made from camel-milk. There had been a cheese-knife stuck into the dull yellow block . . . a knife that was now missing.

The Sheikh frowned again, cocking his head as he slowly glanced back into his stepsister's eyes, then allowing his gaze to move over her body, towards her hands that were still hidden from view.

"You cannot seriously be—"

She was on him before he could finish the sentence, and the Sheikh gasped when he felt the knife drive deep into his pectoral, just below his shoulder blade, missing his jugular by inches but still sending a spray of blood along his white tunic as Maddy pulled the knife back out and with a scream drove toward him again.

But he was ready for her this time, and he grabbed her wrist with one hand, her throat with the other, turning her and grunting as she snapped her teeth in fury, kicked out with her legs and getting him hard on the shins and below the knee. Imraan roared in pain, lifting her full off the floor before slamming her down on the heavy wooden table, knocking the silver cups and porcelain plates off as he pulled her body along the length of the table by her hair.

She screamed and he shouted, and two attendants came bursting into the room. But the Sheikh waved them away without even turning, just shouting "*Abaq beyda 'aw matt!*" to the bewildered men with such authority that they hightailed it out of there almost in relief that they did not have to deal with whatever the hell was happening in here.

"You made me bleed!" the Sheikh gasped as he pulled the knife from her hand and tossed it against the far wall of the room. "You murderous bitch! I am your own family!"

She spat up into his face and laughed, and he slapped her hard on the cheek, grinning when he saw that she spat blood the next time around. Then he pulled her up off the table by her hair, and for one long moment the two of them stared at each other, stepbrother and stepsister, joined not by blood but by something else, something twisted, something old, something neither of them fully understood.

"My family?" she whispered, glancing defiantly at him, her cut lip twisted in a smile, her brown eyes wild with something that almost broke the Sheikh when he recognized it for what it was, what it meant. "Well, that figures. So go ahead, great King. Join the family. Join your father. Take what he took."

Imraan stared at her, a chill running through him as he wondered if she was playing him or if that look in her eye was real. He blinked as he tried to think back to what had happened in that once-happy Royal Palace of theirs, and as the blood flowed from his wound, he could feel tears roll down his cheeks even as she began to sob in his arms.

But neither of their tears were born of sadness, the Sheikh somehow knew. They were tears of hope. Hope that there was a chance . . . a chance to find some answers, answers to questions they'd perhaps never had the courage to truly ask.

"Maddy," he said, touching her broken lip, his fingers trembling as he watched the blood stain his nails. "Ya Allah, Maddy. I am . . . oh, God, I . . . we . . ."

"Please, Imraan," she whispered, glancing at his wound and then into his eyes. "Please."

He could feel her body move beneath his, and he knew his body was reacting to the motion, to the closeness, to the heat. He frowned as he glanced back into her eyes, not sure what she was asking, not sure if he could believe her, believe himself, believe any of it.

"Please, Imraan," she said again. "I know it's sick, I know it's twisted, I know it's wrong. But I need it. I need it right now more than anything, and I know you need it too. It's a part of who I am. It's a part of who you are. Maybe they turned us into the people we are, but that's who we are now. You're the only one who can understand that. Please."

Imraan stared down at her, his head spinning from the loss of blood, the shock of the action, that sensation of guilt he'd felt when he'd seen the truth in her big brown eyes. She was just like him, wasn't she? The product of a family that had done what could never be forgiven. Ya Allah, if only all of them were alive! By God, they would pay! They would pay for what they did to her!

Because she is mine. Mine to protect. Mine to own. Mine to . . . heal.

And so as the sun began to set over the distant sand dunes, casting the land of Wahaad in the shadow of dusk, the Sheikh wiped the blood from his little sister's lips.

Then he leaned in, and he kissed her.

10

The pain of his lips pressing against hers made her moan. She'd always found the pain to be clarifying, the only thing real in a world of fairy-tales and nightmares rolled into one. She remembered focusing on the pain that first time, when her stepfather the supreme Sheikh had entered her chambers, told her what he was going to do, told her it was going to hurt, that it was supposed to hurt. She remembered everything, because suddenly it was like she'd never forgotten.

And just like a switch had been flipped, it all came back as if it had never been buried, never been forgotten: How her mother had held her down that first time, telling her it was her duty. How her stepmother, the first wife and Sheikha of Wahaad had watched from the shadows cast by black velvet curtains. How her own father, her own flesh and blood, hadn't been there to protect her, to save her.

Maddy screamed as she pushed away her own memories, clawing at his hair and wrapping her legs around him as she kissed him furiously. "Please!" she sobbed as she tore at his blood-stained tunic, pulling it off over his head and touching the place she'd stabbed him. He roared in pain, ripping the cloth away from him and stretching his body above hers. She gasped at the sight of his naked torso, his massive chest, broad and glistening, streaked with beautiful red blood, tight dark nipples adorning his pectorals like jewels. His stomach was a mesh of tight muscle, with veins running down along the sides past his hips and disappearing into the waistband of his trousers.

She clawed at his crotch as she unbuttoned him with the other hand, and he grunted and shook his head, grabbing her by the wrists and pulling her arms straight over her head, slamming them against the hard table. She knew she'd have bruises on her knuckles in the morning, and it made her smile.

"I do not trust those hands of yours," he whispered through a half-grin, and she felt her tongue slither out and lick her upper lip as he pressed his swollen crotch against her mound. "They stay where I can see them. Where I can control them."

"We'll see," she whispered, spreading her legs beneath him. Already her gown was up past her hips, and Maddy could feel her wetness drip onto the table as the Sheikh moved on top of her. The tears had dried on her face, and suddenly she was smiling wide. Those memories were still there, but for a moment they felt distant and hollow . . . for a moment: the moment she looked into his green eyes.

Oh, God, is he going to break me completely or put me back together, came the thought as she blinked at what she saw in those green eyes. She almost couldn't bear to let that thought go any further. She could sense the hope at the bottom of it. She could feel the desperation, the yearning, the burning need to find someone who could understand, someone who had been there, someone who could . . . forgive.

Imraan kissed her, and the tears broke again as she turned her face away and shook her head. She couldn't. She wouldn't. He didn't know the twisted details of everything that had happened, and even he would walk away if he did. She couldn't let him in. It was Maddy alone in this cage. Alone. Always and forever.

"Just fuck me," she said, closing her eyes and turning her head as he tried to kiss her again. "Just fuck me, all right?"

She heard his breath catch, his movement stop, his grip on her wrists tighten for a moment before he let go. Then he pulled her up off the table, and she gasped as he lifted her up into his arms like she was a feather. She felt herself being whisked across the room like she was riding on a cloud, and then she felt sunlight on her face, warm air against her bare legs, the smell of fresh palm leaves and the sound of flowing water.

"Make no mistake," he said, his face close to her hair as she leaned against his chest. She could hear his powerful heart beat, and it soothed her. "I will take you when I want, how I want, as often as I want. But first I want to show you something. Come now. Open your eyes."

"No," she whispered, clamping her eyelids down even tighter as she listened to his heart, smelled the desert palms, felt the warm breeze against her ankles and calves. The gurgling of the water was familiar, and it made her stomach lurch as she was taken back to a moment that felt clean, pure, without pain . . . so much so that she didn't want to go back there, didn't want to know that such a place existed within her. Because what if she couldn't stay in that place? She hadn't been able to stay there before, had she?

"Maddy," came his voice, smooth but commanding. "Open your eyes or I will throw you in."

She smiled without meaning to, opening her eyes and blinking in the sunlight filtered through the umbrella-like leaves of desert palms. Then she gasped when she saw it: A desert spring, natural and pure,

bubbling up out of the ground like a miracle. It ended in a pool, serene and perfectly round, surrounded
by palm trees with healthy brown trunks and expan-
sive green leaves.

"Even the cruel desert has its moments of softness
and beauty," the Sheikh whispered against her hair,
kissing her forehead as he held her in his arms like a
doll. "The sand may appear dead, but within it there
is life and hope, Maddy. Life and hope."

The way he said it, the way he kissed her forehead,
the way he held her . . . it all seemed so right that
Maddy almost forgot how twisted it really was. She
clenched her fists as she held on to his strong neck
and back, knowing she had a chance to take a shot at
him again, crash her forehead into his nose, push her
thumbs into his goddamn eyeballs until he screamed
in agony, to pin him down with her powerful legs as
he fell, to strangle him, maybe drown him, like she'd
fantasized about doing to his father at other times,
so many times, when she was too small to stop him
from taking what he wanted, when he wanted.

But he's different, isn't he? He says he's going to
take what he wants, when he wants, but he hasn't
yet, has he? He's come close. So fucking close. But
he's always stopped, like he's waiting . . . waiting
for something. Waiting for me? Waiting for me to
pull up alongside him, to get there with him? Like
we're in this together? Like we've always been in this
together?

"Was it you? It was, wasn't it?" she suddenly said, not knowing why it had suddenly become so clear. Perhaps it was the calmness she saw in his handsome brown face when she finally looked up at him as he kissed her matted hair. Perhaps it was something in the steady rhythm of his heart as she leaned against his rock-hard chest. Or perhaps she was hoping it would be true. "You organized the kidnapping. The first kidnapping. You set it up so my dad would have no choice but to come to you for the money—so much money that there'd be no one else he could turn to."

The Sheikh blinked, and then he shook his head as a chill came over Maddy. Was he lying? She couldn't tell. For the first time, she couldn't read a man. Every man she'd ever met she'd been able to read from the get-go—perhaps because they all wanted the same thing. But this man . . .

"Then who?" she said. "Who would do that? Who *could* do that? Two of my men taken out from a distance, which meant they were professionals. Well trained, and—more importantly—well-paid. Then they take me, throw me in a hole for three days." She paused, shaking her head, still in his arms, the gurgling of the desert spring sounding like thunder as her mind turned with suspicion, swirled with doubt. "And then you show up, Imraan. It had to be you! Why are you lying to me?"

"I would not have had your two men killed just to set this up," the Sheikh said quietly, and instantly she believed him. He would not. She knew it. She wasn't sure how, because at some level she knew he was capable of violence the same way she was, but she knew he was telling her the truth. Still, there was something in his green eyes that made her frown.

"What?" she said, still holding onto him as he stood there beside the spring, beneath the swaying desert palms, under the clear blue sky of day. "What is it?"

"I did not know your two men were killed at long range. How many shots?"

Maddy hesitated. "One shot for each man."

"How close together were the shots?"

"Almost simultaneous," said Maddy, her frown deepening. "Shit, that means there were two shooters. And they coordinated the shots."

Imraan shook his head, his eyes narrowing. "That is military-level discipline. And if the shots were taken at long-range, it is almost certain they were military-trained snipers." He shook his head again. "Ya Allah, that is troubling. Despite what you see in the movies, taking a long-distance shot in the dark and hitting your target the first time takes years of dedicated practice. These were professionally trained snipers who took out your men, Maddy—not some thugs who practice shooting cans in the woods. And professional snipers are not that easy to find. Either they work as highly-paid hitmen—and by highly paid I mean six figures per hit, which seems a bit extreme for taking out two no-name henchmen, no disrespect to your men. Or—"

"That's absurd! My dad doesn't play at that level! We're small-time Atlanta thugs! There's no one in our circles who have those kind of connections, that kind of financing."

"Let me finish," said the Sheikh, almost smiling, though Maddy could tell he was serious as hell. "Or else they work for the government."

Maddy blinked, snorting once and then bursting into laughter against his chest. "OK, now *that's* absurd. How . . . I mean why . . . OK, put me down. I can't have this conversation. It's too surreal."

The Sheikh slowly lowered her to the ground, and Maddy straightened her gown and glanced up at him. She felt a warmth flow through her as she looked up into his eyes, saw his furrowed brow, knew he was puzzling over what was happening just like she was. It was strange, but she felt like they were on the same side now, even though she was technically his captive. Did that make sense? Did any of it make sense?

"Listen," said the Sheikh, looking fiercely at her, not in anger but with an urgency that sent a chill through her body. "Think, Maddy. Did you and your father have any dealings with—"

"With the *government*? Are you insane? We have a tax accountant and a shell business set up just so we can pay enough to the IRS every year that no one bothers us! Hell, we pay tens of thousands in taxes! As for our clients . . . no. There's no way. We're bookies and loan-sharks, Imraan! I knock on people's doors or show up outside their office buildings with my guys to collect the money they lost betting on Braves and Falcons games! Even the mafia offshoots who run book in Atlanta don't give two shits about us! The government? Military snipers? Are you kidding me?"

The Sheikh nodded. "Then there is someone else in this game. Another player. Perhaps more than one."

"Who? And why?"

Imraan snorted. "The why is simple: money. I paid thirty-seven million dollars for you, dear stepsister. That is quite a good reason why." He took a breath. "As for the who . . . now that is more complicated. It has to be someone who knows . . . knows our history. Knows our story. Perhaps knows even more than we do."

Maddy blinked and shook her head. "My father? He's the only one . . . the only one still alive. But—"

"It is beyond your father's imagination. Besides, as you said, he has neither the connections nor the spending habits to pay military snipers to kill his own damn henchmen to fake a kidnapping! No, it is someone else. Another player, Maddy."

Maddy blinked and gritted her teeth. "Yeah, you said that already, Imraan. But who's left? Our mothers are dead, your father is dead, my father is now broke and powerless. Who the fuck is even left in this story? The story of our fucked-up lives? Who else is even left?"

11

"**T**ake a left here," screeched Begum Khalifa as the little Peugeot hatchback turned down a narrow Paris street, tires screeching as the wide-eyed Begum Gaurina grinned like a madwoman behind the wheel, the gold tooth she'd been sporting for the last five years shining like a headlamp. "Slow down before turning! You will kill us both, you wild bitch!"

"We are already dead, remember?" said Gaurina, making the turn at the last minute, the change of direction making both women slide across their seats and hold on for dear life as the car finally skidded to a halt outside the gates of their destination.

"Someday I will teach you the difference between

a metaphor and a goddamn car-crash," Khalifa muttered, pulling the top of her dark-blue hijab over her
hair and checking herself in the rearview mirror. She
scowled at what age had done to her face, glancing
over at the younger and slightly less wrinkled Gaurina in the driver's seat. The two of them didn't drive
themselves around Paris much. They had a Mercedes
Benz limousine and a driver. But tonight's meeting
was private—too private for their talkative West Af-
rican driver, who served the two "dead" Sheikhas in
professional as well as personal capacities and could
not be trusted to keep his mouth shut about anything.

Gaurina laughed, but then went silent as she
straightened her own head covering and fought for
mirror space with Khalifa. Finally they were ready,
and the two old Sheikhas clambered out of their Peugeot hatchback and entered the gates of the nonde-
script house in the Western Suburbs of Paris.

They were searched by two armed men at the door,
and finally they entered the living room. Then they
waited. He always made them wait. They did not
mind. After all, he was their husband. And he was
a king.

He arrived slowly, walking down the wooden stair-
case in his bare feet, his long, well-groomed beard
looking strikingly white against his black silk tunic,
his eyes green and shining, alert and alive as always.
He was old, but he still cast an imposing shadow as

his two queens bowed their heads and waited for him to speak.

"*Laeanaha allh*," he said, glancing at Khalifa and then Gaurina before shaking his head and looking past them, his expression cold and dead, eyes like green stone. "Never again will I trust two women to do a man's job."

Khalifa shifted on her feet, stealing a glance at Gaurina. The younger Sheikha barely moved, her eyes focused on the floor. Khalifa swallowed hard and then raised her head.

"We spared no expense. The men we hired came highly recommended. An ex-military group that specializes in kidnapping. How were we to know they would demand a ransom from Morris instead of simply delivering the girl to you as agreed?" Khalifa said, her voice trembling as she spoke, even though her anger was mostly directed at Gaurina for not speaking up when it was she who'd done most of the planning.

"Ya Allah! Professional kidnappers demanding a ransom! What a surprise! Who would have expected such a thing!" the old Sheikh said, his face twisting into a sneer as he finally deigned to look at his two cowering queens. He took a breath and waved his hand. "I should have known better. I should have done it myself. Perhaps then we would not be—"

"Professionals do not double-cross their employers," said Gaurina suddenly, looking up and pulling her veil and head-covering off, shaking her long black hair open and glaring at the old Sheikh. "There is something else going on here, I swear it. The men we hired asked for a ransom of almost fifty million dollars from Morris! Why would they have done that? They could not possibly have expected he would be able to pay it!"

"But he did pay it. By turning to my son of all people! Ya Allah, I should have you two whipped!" the old Sheikh roared, stretching to full height as his voice thundered across the open space of the old Paris house that was now his palace.

"They *knew* he would have to turn to your son! Somehow they knew!" Gaurina shot back, her dark brown eyes meeting the Sheikh's as Khalifa looked on, pleased that the hot-blooded younger queen was stepping up.

"How? Who knows of our connections besides Morris himself?"

Gaurina went silent, and Khalifa took a breath and spoke. "So perhaps there was no ransom demand at all. Perhaps Morris simply offered to pay them off with a sum so large they could not refuse."

The old Sheikh blinked long and hard. "No," he said. "My instructions were to have the girl taken and brought directly to me. There should have been no contact between the men you hired and Morris. There should have been no way for Morris to even make them an offer."

"So then there is another player," Gaurina said, her

eyes flashing, her lips twisting into a smile. "And you know who it is. There is only one person it can be. Only one other person who knows about what happened twenty years ago. Who knows about us."

The old Sheikh took a long breath and nodded once. "Benson. John Benson. That double-crossing son of a dog. We should have killed him when we had the chance."

"Kill a CIA officer? We would either be dead or kneeling on prayer mats in Guantanamo Bay right now instead of living in Parisian luxury," Khalifa said, her left eyebrow raised, half-smile matching it.

"Luxury? I am a *king!*" roared the old Sheikh, and Khalifa could see the madness in his eyes that had once blazed a fiery green but were now like gray moss on an old rock.

"Our son is king and supreme Sheikh," Khalifa said politely, knowing her calmness would drive her husband's rage even further. She'd always been the steady one of the three, but she also knew how to twist the other two, drive them further than where their own madness might take them, where their own darkness might lead them. "That was the agreement with Benson, and we are bound to it."

The Sheikh closed his eyes and took a long breath. "The girl," he said finally, and when he opened his eyes Khalifa knew she'd won. She'd saved her son by offering Gaurina's daughter as a sacrifice. Give the old man one last taste of power, a throwback to when he owned and possessed everything and everyone, including his own stepdaughter.

The old Sheikh had never touched alcohol, never puffed an opium pipe, never taken so much as an aspirin. Sex and violence—those were his drugs of choice, his paths to pleasure. And all three of them had played those games, were still playing that game.

Sex and violence, Khalifa thought as she looked at her two twisted partners in life. I hope my son has developed different interests, different hobbies, different indulgences.

12

"I never indulge. And I do not keep any in the Royal Palace. But some of the international hotels in Wahaad are allowed to serve alcohol, so I can—"

"All I said is I could use a beer," Maddy said, smiling as she dipped her bare feet in the warm water of the bubbling desert spring. Her white robe was pulled up over her knees, and the Sheikh glanced down at her thighs, feeling himself stiffen again from the sight of his stepsister's smooth skin. "It was just an expression. I don't really want to get drunk, Imraan."

The Sheikh took a breath. It had occurred to him more than once that all of this was indeed an elaborate plan for Maddy and her father to extract money from him. Part of him still believed it was beyond old man Morris's capabilities—and courage—to risk something like this; but it was by no means a closed case. He racked his brain, trying to think back to who else was on the scene twenty years ago, who else could be involved, who else could know secrets that even the two of them did not completely remember.

An image of a man flashed through Imraan's mind. An American, young and confident but also calm, quiet, almost secretive. Imraan had seen him visit the old Sheikh once or twice. He'd thought nothing of it at the time—after all, the Sheikh had hundreds of foreign visitors every year: business dealings, investment opportunities, political negotiations—so why was the memory popping up as if it was an answer to his question?

Do not get carried away, Imraan told himself as he watched Maddy dangle her toes in the clean water coming out of the burning sand. You cannot trust your memories. You cannot trust Morris. And you most certainly cannot trust this woman. What you can trust is reason and logic, and logic dictates that you have to start with what is available to you.

He looked at Maddy again, her long dark hair, light brown neck, strong hips, that beautiful mix of round cheeks and a sharp nose that she'd inherited from her mother.

And then suddenly the Sheikh felt that switch flip

inside him once more, and he saw Gaurina again in his mind, calling to him, reminding him that he was a twisted creature just like she was, just like they all were.

Start with what is available to you, came the thought again. And Maddy is what is available to you. If you are not sure if you can trust her or her father, then first make sure you eliminate that possibility before moving on to the next.

And so just as Maddy turned her head up and smiled, her lips parting as if she was about to say something that reflected the hesitant happiness he could see in her big brown eyes, the Sheikh let that switch flip all the way inside him, that switch that brought on the darkness, turned out the light, took him to that place where anything was possible, the darker the better.

13

She screamed as he grabbed her by the hair and pulled her from where she sat dangling her toes in the warm fresh water. She'd just started allowing herself to relax, to think that perhaps they were going to figure this out together. But then she saw the look on her stepbrother's face, the way his green eyes had lost the hint of warmth and gone stone cold, like a wall had come down between his emotions and his actions.

"You crazy asshole!" she howled as she tried to spin her body around and kick at his knees and legs. But his grip on her hair was tight, down by the roots, and he was dragging her across the sand and then the cobblestone path with such velocity she had to grab

his wrists and allow herself to get pulled along just
so he wouldn't rip her damned hair out!

"Takes one to know one," he muttered as he dragged
her towards the pillars of the outer verandah of the
main palace. He released her for a moment, and she
turned and desperately tried to crawl away and get
to her feet. But he was on her with the quickness of
a snake striking, bringing his knee down on her back
and pushing the air out of her lungs so fast she almost passed out. "And besides, craziness runs in our
family. Especially on your side of the family. It is in
your blood." He leaned in, pushing his knee into her
back as she cried out in pain. "Perhaps I shall let it
out along with your blood. Send you to where your
mother awaits the two of us."

Maddy spat sand from her mouth and blinked as
she gasped for air. Her dead mother awaits the *two* of
them? Why would he say that? The words sent shivers
up her spine, and she blinked again as she saw flashes, snippets of memories, bits and pieces of images
and events. Then suddenly Maddy could see her, a
woman with dark hair and light skin, brown eyes that
flashed with a strange light, full red lips that glowed
bright as they twisted into a smile.

"What do you know about my mother?" she gasped
as she finally stopped struggling just so the Sheikh
wouldn't snap her in half with his power and weight.

"More than I want to know," he grunted, taking the

point of his knee off her and then straddling her from behind so she was pinned down, face against the cobblestones. "Certainly more than I want to remember."

"Well, I don't remember anything about her," Maddy said, taking the deepest breath she could as her mind raced. She could tell that Imraan was on the edge, potentially unhinged, perhaps dangerous even though somehow she didn't feel in true danger for her life. She wasn't sure why, but somehow she still trusted that he wouldn't hurt her . . . hurt her beyond repair, at least. "Help me remember, Imraan. Please."

She felt the Sheikh's thighs tighten as he straddled her, and she swore she sensed movement between his legs. Was it simply his body reacting to being pressed up against hers? Or was it because Maddy had mentioned her mother?

A sudden sickness rose up in Maddy's throat as those images swirled in her head, fragments of color, snippets of sound, words and movement, colors and smells . . . the smell of sex, the color of flesh, the sound of . . .

"Oh, God!" she shouted as she was taken back to that moment, a moment when a little girl peeked through the curtains and saw her mother and her brother in naked embrace, doing things she couldn't understand—or didn't *want* to understand! "Oh,*God*, Imraan! Tell me I'm crazy! Tell me it's just imagination and not memory, that I'm really crazy and delusional!

Please, Imraan! There's no way. There's no goddamn way! There's no way you did that to my mother!"

"She did it to *me*!" he roared from behind her, and in his voice she heard the desperation, the anguish, the unresolved guilt of a boy who'd been forced to become a man before he understood what it meant. "I was thirteen! What in Allah's name was I to do?" He laughed as he gripped her hair from behind, his thighs squeezing her hips, his hardness prominent against her back. "You are just like her, are you not? A crazy whore who deserves to be treated like one. Who *wants* to be treated like one. All right then, daughter of Gaurina. You want to know about your mother? You want to know the kind of woman she was? You want to know what she liked? You will get what you are asking for. By God, you will get what you are asking for."

14

Maddy almost passed out as she felt the fear invade her senses from the inside out. Had she pushed him too far? Had she pushed herself too far? Was he going to fuck her and then kill her? Were those flashes of memory real? Had her mother really seduced the thirteen-year old Imraan, turned him into this sex-crazed beast who was dragging her to his cave by her goddamn hair?

She almost shouted for him to stop, that she was wrong, that she was sorry. She almost told him she understood that at thirteen he was still a child, that even though his body was ready, his mind was not. She almost said those things. Almost.

She held her tongue because somehow she knew this was what he needed, and that she was perhaps the only woman in existence who could give it to him, who could survive it, who could . . . enjoy it?!

Give him what he needs to heal, she thought as she allowed herself to be pulled into the shade of the verandah, the sun disappearing from view as she heard the grunts of the Sheikh, smelled the scent of his shame, sensed her own arousal riding in on waves of fear.

Yes, give him what he needs to heal, she told herself again as she felt him rip her gown down the middle of her back, pull down her panties, slap her naked bottom so hard she gasped in shock, because he is the only one who will eventually give you what you need to heal.

15

"Tell me about my mother," she whispered to him as he stared at her naked buttocks turned up towards him, the remnants of her white gown hanging along her sides like the wings of a broken angel. "Go on, Imraan. Tell me what she liked. What she wanted you to do to her."

He groaned as he felt his cock strain against his pants and underwear, and as his fever rose he unbuckled and unzipped, stripping naked and slapping her ass once again as he felt himself being taken back to a time when the arousal was so all-consuming there was no consideration for right or wrong. But he'd known it was wrong then, and he knew it was wrong now, and he groaned again as he looked down and saw his massive erection spring out in front of him, the head of his cock slapping against Maddy's naked rump as she whispered to him in a voice that sent shivers of dark arousal through his hard body.

What is she doing, he wondered as he ran his hands along her smooth back, rubbing her shoulders, kneading her buttocks, reaching around her and pressing her breasts until she rounded her back and pushed her ass against his cock. What is she doing to me? Is she playing me like her mother did? Seducing me like her mother did? Breaking me like her mother did?

Or is she trying to put me back together?

He could feel the sickness rise up in him, but along with it came that all-consuming arousal, a need so overwhelming he roared in anguish as he tried to fight it, to push away the memories that were flooding his mind, memories that Maddy had brought with her.

"Please," she whispered, turning her head sideways and glancing at him. The shadows cast by the pillars of the verandah made her face look dark, beautiful, different. "Please," she said again to him, nodding. "I need it too, Imraan. It's the only way to set us both free. Let go. Let loose. For both of us. Please."

He pushed his middle finger into her asshole as she spoke, and she gasped, her breath catching in her throat as the Sheikh felt the last bit of self-restraint leave him. He no longer gave a damn if she was playing him, if she was drawing him in so she'd have another chance to slit his throat. He didn't give a damn anymore. He was too far gone.

"Call me by her name," she whispered as he pumped two fingers into her rear hole and rubbed the head of his cock against her slit from beneath, feeling their juices mix as her wetness flowed down along his glistening shaft. "I am her, Imraan. Live it out once more. Live it out, and then let it go."

The Sheikh felt tears roll down his face as his arousal grew. His mind was a squirming coil of images and emotions, his eyes unfocused and useless. He could hear himself panting like an animal, groaning like a beast, muttering like a madman. He could feel her move her buttocks against him as he fingered her anus and teased her vagina. He wanted to let go. He wanted to let go of it all, always and forever. Was this the way? Was she the way?

The thoughts swirled and twisted as his vision clouded over again, and then he felt her hands reach between her thighs and grasp his balls, massaging them and slowly pulling him forward until his cockhead was firmly pressed against her entrance, opening her wide, her heat feeling like fire against his swollen tip.

"Ya Allah," he groaned as he curled his fingers inside her ass and began to push his thick shaft into her. "Ya Allah . . . Gaurina! My father will have us both killed if he finds out. My mother will die of shame if this becomes known."

"And we will deserve it," she whispered back as she spread her thighs and pulled him by his heavy balls until he could resist no longer and rammed himself all the way into her so hard she screamed.

"Then we had better make it worth it," he growled as he pulled his fingers out of her asshole, grabbed her hair with one hand, her throat with the other, and began to pump with everything he had in him, all of it, twenty years worth.

"Oh, God! Oh, *fuck*!" she howled, bracing herself against the floor, her fingers clawing against the thick Persian rug as the Sheikh's thrusts slammed his hips against her cushion so hard he could see the bruises forming on her smooth buttocks.

Still he pumped, roaring as he felt something inside him snap, like a lever had been released, a switch flipped. "Can you take it?" he muttered, his lips moving as if by some unknown force, the words spewing out of him like he'd said them before. "Am I too big for you, Gaurina? Too strong for you, my Sheikha? Am I ruining you . . . ruining you for my father? Stretching you so wide he will never be able to pleasure you again?"

His own words shocked him, but they were coming from so deep inside he couldn't stop them. He knew he was crying, and he smiled as the tears rolled down his cheeks and onto her shuddering buttocks as he pumped into her, drawing back and driving forward with such force he could feel his own ass and hamstrings flex to their limit. But she took everything he gave, screaming and howling as he pounded into her, coaxing him on when he wasn't sure if she could handle it.

And then finally, as she grasped his balls and led him into a climax so strong he almost passed out on top of her, she turned her tear-streaked face and looked at him and whispered: "Your father . . . your father already has something new to give him pleasure."

The Sheikh's eyes suddenly snapped into full focus just as he felt himself explode into his stepsister's valley, flooding her with his seed as he looked into her eyes. And in those eyes he saw the same madness he felt flowing through his climaxing body, saw the same darkness that had twisted her inside and out, the same desperate plea: That perhaps he was her only chance, her only hope, her only path out of hell and into . . . into whatever this was.

And what is this, by God, he wondered as he flexed inside her, pushing out the last of his semen and then collapsing on top of her, pushing her face-down to the carpet with his weight. Is this a path out of the darkness or are we going deeper into it?

He lay on top of her for several long moments, his mind still processing what she'd said to him. She'd said it before: daring him to take what his father had taken from her. But he hadn't made the connection, hadn't fully taken it in. But now he knew it was true. And somehow he knew that it had fueled Gaurina's fire as well.

He kissed her matted hair, smelled her sweet perspiration, and suddenly Imraan knew that something had changed inside him. He felt a strange lightness, an inner warmth, a feeling of intensity for this woman beneath him. Suddenly he wanted to protect her, to heal her, to bring her out of the psychological pit in which she'd been living since she was a child. But how? How in Allah's name could he bring her out?

And then he knew the answer. He'd have to do for her what she did for him. He'd have to descend into her darkness, just like she'd descended into his. He'd have to go down to those depths and bring her back with him. Give her what she needed, just like she gave him what he needed.

But what does she need? How can I heal what my father broke in her? How can I get back what her own parents—*our* parents—took from her when she was too young to stop them, too innocent to protest, too small to fight back?

Imraan looked into Maddy's eyes as he thought, and the answer came in the way she looked back at him. That steady look, unwavering, firm, focused. Those same eyes that had seen him with her own mother through the curtains. Those same eyes that had seen the old Sheikh do what a man can never be forgiven for doing. Those same eyes that were looking at him now.

Ya Allah, she does not need to act out the past, re-enact what broke her. I needed it because I had forgotten. But she never forgot in the same way I did. She never carried the same kind of guilt I did. So she will not need what I needed. She needs the opposite. She does not need to remember or re-live. She needs to forget . . . forget that her childhood was stolen, her innocence corrupted, her trust violated by the very people who were supposed to protect her with their lives, love her unconditionally, always and forever.

That is what she needs, the Sheikh thought as he stroked her hair, kissed her lips, watched her blink in surprise at his sudden gentleness. I have spanked her, choked her, slapped her. I have pushed her face against the carpet, slid my fingers into her rear, fucked her with all the power and rage I had in me. Now I need to love her. I need to love her like she's never been loved, hold her like she's never been held, kiss her like she's never been kissed. I need to be everything and everyone to her—everyone who betrayed her. I need to be her father, her brother, her lover, her best friend—everything she has never had, things she believes she does not deserve to have. But I don't need to say those things. I just need to *be* them. Everything and everyone.

He touched her cheek, her broken lips, caressed

her neck as she sighed and looked up at him, that puzzled expression in her eyes becoming clearer, like the sun trying to break through the black clouds of a winter storm.

The next move you make is a commitment, the Sheikh thought as he took a breath and glanced at her full lips, her wide eyes, her soft round cheeks. If she trusts you and you betray her, she will be beyond repair. So think carefully before you head down this path, Imraan, he told himself. Will you see this through? Do you trust*yourself* enough to head down this path? Because it will not last one night or one week or one month. It will last forever.

"Please," she whispered, looking up at him and nodding, and even though neither of them could be sure what she was asking for, the Sheikh nodded back and smiled down at her.

Then he kissed her. For the first time, he truly kissed her.

16

She'd been fucked by men as far back as she could re-member, taken every which way until it didn't even matter, until it felt like nothing. She'd taken lovers when she felt the need over the years, using them and tossing them aside like trash when they couldn't give her what she needed. But she'd never been kissed. Not like this. Not like it meant something. Not like it meant . . . everything.

"What is wrong with us?" she whispered as she opened her mouth to receive his kiss. "Oh, God, what is wrong with us?"

"A lot," he said, breaking from the kiss and grinning down at her. "But we will fix it. One kiss at a time."

She smiled back, feeling a lightness enter her as the Sheikh's lips pressed against hers, his warm tongue entering her mouth as he pressed his full weight down on her, his chest squishing her boobs, his hips spreading her legs, his hardness lining up perfectly against her slit.

"You remember everything, do you not?" he whispered as he ran his palms down her naked sides, gripping her buttocks and pressing hard as she moved beneath him.

She nodded, arching her back as he kissed her neck. "I didn't for a long time. Not clearly, even though I knew it was there, buried, or behind a wall or something. But something happened over the past few days, ever since I met you, and now I remember him: Your father. I wish I didn't, but yes, I remember. Every moment. Every fucking moment."

Maddy felt a sliver of electricity rip through her like fire as she fought the memories, and she dug her nails into his back as she tried to control the rage that so often felt uncontrollable. She felt the Sheikh tighten, and she knew she'd drawn blood with her nails. But he remained calm, still caressing her, still kissing her gently, still moving slowly over her, his body like a protective blanket over her damaged psyche.

"Do you want to forget?" he whispered against her cheek even as she dragged her nails along his back, feeling his skin tear from the anger she was trying to control. "Do you want to forget it all, Maddy?"

"I . . . I don't know," she muttered, sliding her hand into his thick hair, moving her wide open hips against his growing hardness, feeling her wetness ooze as that dark arousal rose up in her, sending shivers down her back, past her naked buttocks, through her thighs, down to her toes. "I may not have had the memories until now, but I had the emotions. All that anger, all that hatred . . . it's protected me all these years. If I let that go . . ."

"Then what will protect you? Is that what scares you? You'll lose the source of your strength? The fuel that allows you to do what you do?"

She blinked, her eyes going wide, her grip on his hair loosening, her nails stopping their violent journey across his broad back. "Maybe. Yes. I don't know. I just haven't—"

"*I* will protect you," he whispered fiercely against her neck. "I will do what I should have done twenty years ago and protect the girl who couldn't protect herself. It was my responsibility. I failed then. I will not fail now."

"But you didn't know back then," she said, frowning up at him. "You were a child too, Imraan. You didn't know what was happening behind those closed doors, those drawn curtains."

"Perhaps I did, Maddy. Maybe that's why I shut down, locked away *all* the memories of that time. Maybe it had nothing to do with what happened between your mother and me. Maybe the guilt and self-hatred that's driven me all these years had nothing to do with her and everything to do with you, the girl I couldn't protect."

She searched his face, a face familiar but yet that of a stranger. They weren't related by blood, but in a way it was flesh and blood that bound them together, that created them, twisted them into what they'd become.

"I don't need your protection," she said, smiling up at him.

"Really?" he said. "Your men were shot dead as they stood beside you. You were kidnapped, and then sold by your own father."

"He sold me to *you*!" she said, almost laughing as she looked into his eyes that were full of mischief. "And he did it to protect me."

"So then you do need protection. And how is it you are defending your father suddenly? The man is a monster, Maddy. Any man who would—"

"My father never touched me," she said suddenly. "Not like that, at least." She took a breath, her eyes closing as her lips trembled. When she opened her eyes again, she could feel the change come across her. Her guard was up, her mind retreating back to her fortress, her gates closed off as quickly as they had opened for the Sheikh. "Not like your father did."

"But your father allowed it. He knew, did he not? How could he not have known?"

Maddy took a breath, her eyes getting back that cold, dead focus that had gotten her through hell, allowed her to survive the unthinkable, the deepest of betrayals. "They must have known. All of them. All four of them. I was still young, but you were older. Don't you remember? How can you not remember? You were there, Imraan. You were there, and . . . and . . ."

She swallowed as she felt a lump in her throat, and the anger rose as she told herself she wasn't going to cry, she wasn't going to break. Big girls didn't cry. Tough girls didn't break.

She watched as a shadow passed across like the Sheikh's handsome face like the sun going behind a cloud, and she could see his green eyes lose focus as if he was trying to remember. Or perhaps he was trying to forget. It didn't make sense. How could he not remember?!

"I don't remember, but I must have known. And I didn't protect you," he whispered, closing those green eyes as he bowed his head, his forehead touching hers. "Instead I gave in to her, to your mother. I indulged myself while you were . . . while they . . . ya Allah, I wish they were alive. By God, I wish they were alive so I could tear them all apart, rip their cold hearts out with my goddamn hands! How could they, Maddy? How could they?!"

She just shook her head and smiled. She paused

for a moment, the next sentence coming out in a low whisper. "I'm asking myself that as well. And also the question I know you're asking yourself: If these are our parents, then what hope do we have?"

"Genetics is not destiny," the Sheikh said fiercely, his eyes focusing on hers, their gaze locked. "You are not your mother, and I am not my father."

Maddy laughed, the sound coming out hollow as she looked up into his green eyes. "Who was my mother? Who was your father? Our memories are disjointed and chaotic, bits and pieces of events and emotions. The only thing clear is that I hated them. And you say you don't remember much more than what you've told me!"

The Sheikh frowned, and Maddy swore she saw that shadow cross his face again. Did he remember and was he lying? Was it just repression? Was it the guilt of knowing that his stepsister was being abused while he fucked his stepmother? Or was there something else that had made him forget? It did seem strange that he would forget so much, didn't it? That both of them would forget so much, only to have it come back in sudden spurts after they were reunited?

"Maddy, I barely even remembered your mother until you came back into my life," he whispered. "It does not make sense. I do not drink. I have never done drugs. For the most part my mind is clear, focused, sharp. But when I try to go back there, back to that time, it is like a black hole, a wall, a door with a lock on it."

Maddy nodded. "That's how it's been for me too. I remember all the pain, all the emotion, all the horror. But I can't get to the details. I don't understand why. I can't remember *why*!"

"So then we will have to ask the only person still alive who might have the answers," the Sheikh said. "Your father."

Maddy snorted. "OK. You want his number?"

The Sheikh smiled. Then he rose up off her and reached for his phone, punching in a number and stretching his naked body as he spoke. "*Jalb aleisabat alqadimata*," he said quietly. "*Afealha alan*."

Maddy frowned as she watched him toss the phone aside and return to her. "What the hell was that?" she asked.

"Your father will be brought here within twenty-four hours. He will answer every question, and he will answer truthfully. I guarantee it."

Maddy's eyes widened as she processed what he was saying. "Wait, you're having my father kidnapped? You're going to bring him here and threaten to torture him if he doesn't answer all our questions?"

Imraan shrugged, that darkness glowing in his green eyes in a way that reminded Maddy of the twisted blood that flowed through his veins. His and hers. Genetics might not be destiny, but it was certainly something. Something dark. Something . . . exciting?

"Perhaps I will torture him anyway," the Sheikh said. "Even if he does answer all our questions. How do you feel about that, little stepsister?" he whispered to her, pressing his body against hers as she felt her arousal ratchet up so fast she almost passed out. What kind of people were they? Were they any better than the monsters who'd spawned them?

She looked up at him as she spread her legs and pushed her mound up against his hardness. Then she leaned up and kissed him full on the lips. "I feel like . . . like that's so . . . romantic. So fucking romantic."

17

This kiss was different. Deeper. Darker. It meant something, just like the last kiss had, but the meaning scared her. If genetics wasn't destiny, what was destiny? What had brought them together after twenty years? Two abused step-siblings, joined not by their own blood but by blood nonetheless?

Maddy could feel the blood on his back as she ran her fingers along his muscled shoulder-blades, the ripples on his back feeling like a pit of snakes, all intertwined, no telling where one began and the other ended. She kissed the wound on his front pectoral, where she'd stabbed him with a goddamn cheese-knife, licking the blood and smiling as he smothered her lips with a ferocious kiss that was as hot as it was cold. She could feel the soreness from the way he'd fucked her less than an hour ago, tasted her own blood from her broken lip mix with his even as their saliva mixed while he rubbed the head of his cock against her wet mound. They were sick, she knew. They were wrong, she was certain. They were in love, she decided.

They were in love, she told herself as she licked her lips and stretched her arms wide as he pulled off the remnants of her white gown, pressed her heavy breasts so hard she could see the marks left by his fingers, took her peaked red nipples into his mouth and sucked so hard she screamed.

Yes, they were in love, she thought again as she watched him kiss her naked stomach, lick her belly-button until she giggled, then bury his face in her dark triangle of brown curls, pushing his nose through her forest and breathing deep of her scent in a way that made her shudder as she spread for him.

Of course they were in love. They had to be: There was no one else either of them could love, and nobody else that could love either of them. After all, if you're spawned by monsters, then where else are you going to find love except with your own kind?

18

He felt her come all over his face as he inhaled deep of her feminine musk, opening his mouth wide and drinking her nectar as he flicked her clit with his tongue, spread the dark lips of her cunt with his fingers and pushed his nose and mouth as deep into her as he could. He held her down by her thighs as she came, watching her wetness flow like a river as he kissed her perineum, fingered her rear hole, kneaded her buttocks until her shuddering slowed to a steady, calm shiver.

"I love you, Maddy," he whispered as he felt the pain from the stab-wound rip through him as she touched him there. He knew she'd ripped open the skin on his back with her claws, and he smiled as she caressed his torn shoulder-blades, spreading his own blood over him like an ointment. Of course he loved her. He'd always loved her. Just like he'd always loved her mother.

The thought came to him so casually it almost made him choke, and even though the Sheikh knew he was aroused beyond belief, bleeding and in pain, obviously not thinking clearly, it made sense in a way. How could he not love a woman who'd made a teenage boy's every fantasy come true? It was rape. It was wrong. It was twisted. But it was . . . family.

He moved up from between her legs, lining up his massive, throbbing cockhead with his stepsister's warm slit, kissing her full on the mouth.

"Taste yourself," he muttered as he licked her lips and watched her smile. "How do you taste?"

"Kinda salty," she muttered, half-smiling as her eyelids fluttered open. "I should probably take a bath."

The Sheikh raised an eyebrow and nodded. "That is an excellent idea."

Maddy opened her mouth wide. "Excuse me?! I've never been so insulted in my entire life!"

The Sheikh grunted. "Well, you are still young. Come on. Up we go."

She squealed like a girl as he lifted her off the carpet, gathering her in his arms, his erection bouncing as he strode out past the open verandah and toward that bubbling desert spring beneath the open skies of the kingdom of Wahaad. It was just the two of them, and although the Sheikh tried to think of memories of just the two of them as children, playing together like children should, there were no such memories to be found.

We will make those memories, he decided as he grinned at her pretty round face, laughed at the way she grabbed his hair and threatened to kill him if he threw her in. Ya Allah, we will *make* those memories! We might be the children of monsters, and perhaps there is no escape from that. But we can also be the children we never really got a chance to be. The friends that we perhaps were but the memories of which were corrupted and twisted by those that we trusted and loved. The lovers that perhaps we were destined to be, always and forever.

And so he kissed his little Maddy one last time on the mouth, and as she squealed in delight like a child at a water-park, he tossed her head-first into the warm pool created by the clean waters that bubbled up from the mysterious depths of the Wahaadi desert.

Then, just as she came up the first time for air, gasping and threatening bloody murder, the beads of water rolling off her body like pearls, her breasts looking like golden dunes in a summer rainstorm, he jumped in alongside her, grabbing her by the waist and pulling her beneath the surface.

He held her there for a few seconds, looking at her through the clear water. She was calm, smiling, staring back at him as if she understood what was happening, as if she realized that in this moment they were taking control of their lives, choosing to be born again, baptized by their own choices, one choice in particular:

The choice to be together.

19

The warm waters flooded her senses as she went under, but he was there beside her the moment she sank. Perhaps he'd always been there beside her—or at least wanted to be there, even when he was too young to stop what was happening. She gasped as she felt the Sheikh's strong arms slide around her waist, holding her upright against his body in the shallow pool.

He pushed two fingers up inside her as she pressed her ass against him, and she moaned as he drove them in and out, his hardness expanding against her rear crack as he leaned in and whispered, "Do you feel clean now, Maddy?"

She shook her head, arching her neck back as the

Sheikh fingered her hard, his thumb rubbing her clit roughly. "Not yet," she groaned. "I think you missed a spot. A little to the left. There we go. Oh, shit, Imraan. Oh, *fuck*, that feels so good."

She could feel him flex his cock against her rear entrance as he fucked her with his finger, and she moved her ass left to right as she let him line his cockhead against her rear pucker. She did feel clean, she realized as the warm, waist-high waters lapped against her stomach. The sun was hot on her shoulders, the breeze lazy and slow. There were no witnesses but the distant sand dunes, the silent minarets of the empty palace. It was just the two of them, and in that moment Maddy understood that here they could be anyone they wanted to be, that they weren't bound by what had happened to them, by the choices made by others. They could make their own choices, forget the past, cleanse themselves of everything that had happened. Perhaps it could be as simple as that!

But then she heard the Sheikh grunt against her, slide a third finger inside her as he massaged her rear entrance wide open with his masthead, muttering in Arabic, his breath warm against her cheek. Her arousal was spiraling upwards, and she was about to come again when suddenly she thought the sun was blinding her, the waters burning her flesh, the sand dunes closing in and smothering her.

"No," she groaned as she felt her climax start to roll

in like distant thunder, those dark memories rolling in alongside. "Please, Sheikh. No. No. *No!*"

But still he pushed his cock against her, his fingers driving into her cunt with fury. He was two inches deep, the head of his cock inside her anus, her climax thundering in like a stampede of Arabian wildhorses when her vision narrowed to a single point, her eyes rolled up in her head, and all she could see were the faces of the two queens, one holding her down, the other watching from the shadows, both of them smiling, both of them laughing, both of them nodding.

"Take her like the little whore she is," said Begum Khalifa.

"Show her who is Sheikh of the land," said Begum Gaurina.

"Open her wide with your royal manhood," said Begum Khalifa.

"Ruin her for every other man, your Highness," said Begum Gaurina.

"*No!*" she howled, pulling away from him, feeling the suction as his cock popped out of her asshole like a cork. She whipped around, the water flying all around them as she brought her arm around, hand balled in a fist, eyes closed. "I'll kill you!"

She felt him grab her by the wrist, and she howled in despair as he spun her back around and pushed her forward. Then suddenly her head was underwater, and she gurgled as her eyes opened wide, her mouth taking in water as she felt the Sheikh's tremendous strength overpower her. Now she was that little girl again, alone and powerless, betrayed by those who were supposed to protect her, and for a moment she wanted to just breathe deep and let the warm water end it all, finish this story for her. There wasn't going to be a happy ending, was there? She'd been betrayed by her mothers, raped by her stepfather, sold by her real father. Now her stepbrother owned her, and he had her face-down and underwater, about to remind her whose son he was, about to remind her who the Sheikh of the land was, about to prove to both of them that perhaps genetics was indeed destiny, that there was no escaping who they were.

She took another gulp of the sweet water, feeling herself begin to lose consciousness, a sickening calmness entering her as she felt the Sheikh spread her rear cheeks beneath the surface of the tranquil pool. It would be so easy to give up, to give in, to let go. So fucking easy.

But then she lifted her head out of the water with a gasp, spitting and screaming at the same time. She wasn't going to give up, and she was never going to give in. No one could do anything to her that hadn't been done. Either she was broken beyond repair, or she could never, ever be broken. Which meant it didn't fucking matter. She was in charge, not he—no matter what he did.

"Do it," she snarled, spreading her ass and pushing back against him. "Do it, you sick fuck. Prove to me whose son you are, great Sheikh. Prove to me that we're part of the same fucked-up family. Remind me that I'm your little whore and you're the big man who controls the realm and everyone in it."

20

Once upon a time I controlled a realm and everyone in it, thought the old Sheikh as he watched his two queens bow their heads and slowly exit the room. I was master, lord, king. A God upon this Earth. And now I am an exile, a man with no name, a king with no kingdom. Ya Allah, I want that feeling one more time before I die. That feeling of being in total control, that sense of absolute power, of being above the laws of common morality.

And there is only one way to regain that feeling, to experience that unbridled high, to remind myself that I am a God who walks on Earth. Just one way to taste the sweetness of what I had twenty years ago.

I am too old and tired to attempt to rule again, and politics was never that interesting to me anyway. The real taste of power came to me in other ways, and I want to feel that sweetness again. There is only one way. One person. The girl.

The girl. That little innocent I turned into a whore to show them all who was in charge. The girl who is ultimately responsible for my situation today, even though she does not know it.

The girl.

One last taste, and I will leave this world behind. Yes, I will leave this world behind, the old Sheikh thought as he traced his fingers along the jeweled hilt of the old dagger he always carried, but I will not exit alone. The girl will come with me to the next world. We are bound together, our fates intertwined just like our bodies were twenty years ago.

His thoughts drifted back to the present as he dropped his dark robes over the dagger. The girl was with his son now, the new Sheikh of the land, the new lord of the old realm. Imraan, that little dog. What did he remember? What did he know? And what would he do?

21

What will you do, Imraan, came the thought as the Sheikh felt the arousal almost take over while he looked down through the clear waters at her round buttocks spread before him. There was a sense of power in the moment that was intoxicating, almost overwhelming. He was king, was he not? He could take what he wanted, do what he wanted, finish what he started. He could show her who he was, show*himself* who he was!

She was taunting him, teasing him, daring him. He had no choice but to do it, yes? Hold her down, push himself forward, and finish it. No choice.

Imraan looked down at himself, his manhood stretched long and hard beneath the surface of the water, Maddy bent forward and spread before him, gasping for air. What choice was he making here? What choices were they both making? Destiny? Genetics? The son of the father? The daughter of the mother?

No, he suddenly thought as he watched her turn her head and taunt him again, her eyes filled with tears. I have to make the choice for both of us. It is my responsibility to fix what my father broke. It is the only way to free us both. It is my choice, and mine alone. I am a king, and I choose my destiny.

And then he grabbed her by the shoulders and pulled her up as she spat water and took deep gulps of air. He spun her around to face him, smiling as those fists of hers came around with her and got him square on the cheek. He would have a black eye in an hour, but it did not matter. He had chosen his destiny, and she was it.

"Maddy," he shouted, taking one more blow from her flying fists and then grabbing her wrists before she broke his nose. "I am sorry. Maddy, listen. I am sorry. I am sorry!"

He lifted her out of the water as she began to sob, cradling her in his arms like the broken child she was in that moment. Just in that moment though, because the Sheikh understood that just like she'd never had the chance to be a child, she'd never truly been broken. Damaged but not broken.

He carried her out of the pool as the sun shone

down on them. Water rolled off their naked bodies in beads, blood oozed from the Sheikh's cuts and wounds, tears flowed from Maddy's eyes. It was like their bodies were expelling their pasts, clearing the way for something new, something fresh, something clean.

The Sheikh kissed her forehead as he laid her down under the shade of a desert palm, her body cradled against his. They stayed there in silence, the warm desert breeze drying their bodies as the hot sun shone in splinters through the deep green palm leaves. He stroked her hair, kissed her face, held her close like he knew she needed, like he knew *he* needed. Slowly he could feel the warmth of the desert elements take root in them, and he realized she was no longer crying, he was no longer bleeding, and they were both smiling.

Then she glanced up at him with those big brown eyes, the eyes of a woman reborn. "So I was just wondering," she whispered, and in those eyes he could see a strange mix of light along with that old darkness, like there was a balance coming into play, a balance that would perhaps sustain them for the rest of their lives. "How do I taste now?"

22

He tasted her again and again as she came for him, and their laughter filled the air like birdsong as they rolled around beneath the swaying palm trees. Their bodies were covered in fine golden sand, their hair matted and twisted, their skin glowing with perspiration.

After he made her come for the third time with his mouth, the Sheikh took her back to that gurgling pool, washing the sand off her face and body as she stroked him to a hardness that almost made him choke. Then he held her upright and took her, slowly and carefully, pushing himself up into her with long, powerful strokes as she spread for him beneath the desert waters.

They came together, brother and sister, their cries of ecstasy merging with the sound of flowing water. And when they were done Maddy looked into Imraan's eyes and kissed his lips and sighed.

"This is only the beginning, isn't it?" she whispered.

"I certainly hope so," he replied. "I certainly hope so."

23

"**B**ack to the beginning, Morris," snarled the Sheikh, taking slow steps around the old man tied to a chair. "I want the full story. All of it. Every last detail, no matter how twisted."

Morris took a long breath as he glanced at his bound wrists, tested the bonds on his ankles. He was old but strong, and the Sheikh knew better than to underestimate a man who'd survived in the American underworld for thirty years.

"You think I'm scared of this bullshit act you're putting on?" Morris replied coolly. "What the fuck are you going to do to me? I'm already broke, wiped out. You've taken my daughter. What else is left? My life?

Go ahead and take it. In fact, hand me a gun and I'll pull the trigger myself. Who gives a shit."

"I give a shit," came her voice from the left, and Morris turned and blinked in the dim light of the windowless store-room beneath the kitchens of the Royal Palace.

"Maddy?" he said. "You're . . ." He glanced at the Sheikh and then back at his daughter, a tight smile showing on his lips before his expression went stoic again.

"Alive? Did you think I was going to kill her?" the Sheikh asked, frowning as he tried to read the old man's expression. "I gave you my word, did I not?"

Morris closed his eyes, that tight smile coming back for a moment before disappearing again. "I have nothing to say to either of you. What's done is done. The past should stay in the past. Trust me, there's nothing to be gained by going back to what happened twenty years ago."

"We will decide what's to be gained," said the Sheikh, taking a step closer as he felt his blood rise. His memories of this man were still hazy, and he could sense something rippling beneath the surface. Why in Allah's name couldn't he remember clearly? He was old enough at the time. What had they done to him?

"You don't remember, do you, boy?" said Morris almost like he could read the Sheikh's thoughts, and Imraan blinked as the old man opened his eyes and glanced up. "Of course not. They did a number on you. On both of you. Military-grade hypnosis." He laughed and shook his head. "Hell, I wish they'd done it on all of us. It would have made things so much easier! We could have forgotten all that shit instead of carrying it with us for two decades." He snorted, glancing at Maddy and then looking down. "Though perhaps that was why he didn't mess with all our memories. He wanted the rest of us to remember. That self-righteous piece of shit."

Imraan blinked rapidly, his eyelids fluttering as a fleeting image of that other man—the young American in a black suit—came back and then disappeared. "Who? Speak, Morris. Do not underestimate me. I will make you talk, one way or the other." The Sheikh glanced over at Maddy and then back at Morris. "One way or the other."

Panic flashed across the old man's face when he looked at his daughter, saw her swollen lip, the bruises on her upper arms. He looked back at Imraan, frowning as if he was trying to figure out whether the Sheikh was bluffing. After all, Maddy was standing free in the center of the room, not in shackles in the corner.

"You're bluffing," Morris finally said, his jaw tightening as he looked away from his daughter and into the Sheikh's eyes. "You don't have it in you. You didn't then, and you don't now."

The Sheikh took a long breath, filling his lungs as he felt an anger rise up in him like the tide coming in. Slow and steady, but unstoppable in its power. He turned and nodded, glancing at Maddy and narrowing his eyes at her. Then with two long strides he closed the distance between them and grabbed her by the hair, pulling her down to her knees as she screamed in real shock.

She tried to turn and swing at him, but Imraan pushed her face-down onto the floor, driving his knee into her back and holding her down. Then he reached behind his back and pulled out the curved dagger with the jeweled hilt that had been part of a set— the second of which was missing. He held the edge of the blade to Maddy's left ear, glancing up at her father and holding the eye contact without so much as a single blink.

"I do not have it in me? You know whose son I am. You know whose blood runs in my veins. So now decide, old man. Talk, or I make you talk."

The Sheikh could feel Maddy's panic as she tightened beneath his weight. He could tell that even she wasn't certain if he was bluffing or not. But the worst of it, the part that scared him the most, the part that made his blood run cold was that Imraan himself wasn't sure if he was bluffing. He could feel that internal wall coming down again, and suddenly those moments he'd shared with Maddy seemed like a childish dream, something that was part of another person's life, something that wasn't real, was too far away to be real.

"Imraan," Maddy gasped as the blade touched the back of her ear. "You're insane. He doesn't give a shit about me. He'll let you cut me up into a hundred pieces before he breaks."

Imraan ignored her, staring down Morris as he watched the old man's eyebrows twitch. "You are the only thing this man cares about," he said quietly. "He handed over the spoils from a life of crime, went down on his knees to beg me for a loan, and agreed to my every demand just to save you from whoever kidnapped you to begin with. Which means he *knows* who kidnapped you in the first place, and he knows that whatever I might do to you would pale in comparison to what they would have done. So talk, old man. I know you give a damn about her, and I know she is the only thing keeping that light going in your eyes."

Morris glanced at his daughter, and back at the Sheikh. Then he shook his head, smiled, and finally nodded. "You give a damn about her too, Imraan. But you aren't bluffing, are you?"

"No," said the Sheikh, that feeling of horror at what he was prepared to do coming in so strong his hand began to shake. "I am not. I promised you I would not kill her, but that is all I promised you."

"All right, you goddamn madman!" Morris said, his eyes finally going wide as he strained against his bonds. "Put that dagger down. I'll tell you what I know." He took a breath and closed his eyes, his head shaking as he exhaled. When he opened his eyes there were tears. "But I should warn you, once you hear it all, there's no unhearing it. No going back."

24

Maddy spun away from Imraan the moment he released her, and it took all her willpower to not descend on him with everything she had. He was going to cut her fucking ear off? He was a goddamn psycho!

But her father had started talking, and she gathered herself and listened, glancing over at Imraan one last time before deciding that she needed to be done with this family once and for all. Both of them. There was only one way out, and that meant only one person was going to be leaving this room when all was said and done.

She glanced at that dagger hanging loose in the Sheikh's hand, the blood chilling in her veins when she realized what she was thinking. In three steps she could get there, snatch that blade from his hands, slash his throat with a swift upward strike. She wouldn't even need to do anything to her father. She could just leave him there. There'd been no attendants down here as far as she knew. The Sheikh had brought her father down to this windowless room on his own. He was old and weak. How long would he last? He wouldn't even starve to death: he'd run out of oxygen in about a day in this closed box!

Maddy almost staggered, and she took a deep breath when she realized she'd been holding her breath as these sickening thoughts took root in her mind. As she exhaled she heard her father's voice, and she finally tuned in and listened.

"I met Gaurina at a club in London," he said. "She was young, exotic, and mesmerizing. I couldn't get enough. Hell, she certainly couldn't get enough."

Maddy watched as Imraan's body tightened, but she said nothing. Neither did the Sheikh.

"I had no idea who she was. If I'd known, I'd have stayed the hell away." Morris shook his head and looked down. "Begum Gaurina. The second wife of the Sheikh of Wahaad. A man with a reputation for brutality. A man who'd reinstated punishments like stoning to death, amputation, and public beheadings. A man who'd decreed that the legal age for marriage was thirteen." He snorted and glanced up at Imraan. "Your father."

Imraan took a breath, his green eyes narrowed and focused. "I know," he said. "Go on."

"We spent six weeks together in Europe, and she was pregnant by the end of it. I wanted to marry her, bring her back to America. I told her she'd love Atlanta—after all, the weather would suit her, I used to joke." Morris smiled and shook her head. "And then she told me who she was, told me she was already married, told me that she was taking my baby back to Wahaad and there wasn't a damned thing I could do about it."

"Why? Why would she want to do that?" Imraan asked, looking at Maddy and then back at Morris. "It would have been suicide to show up at my father's door with another man's child."

"Obviously it wasn't," Morris said, his eyes narrowing now too as he met the Sheikh's gaze. "And you know why."

Maddy watched as the Sheikh took a breath, and she could feel her head spin as those memories assaulted her like bullets in the darkness of the room. Memories of her own mother holding her down that first time, smiling like a witch as the old Sheikh descended on her like an angry god.

"Tell me why," Imraan said, and Maddy could see his rage. Suddenly she was reminded of that moment when he swore he'd protect her, that it was his responsibility to protect her when no one else would. What part of him could she believe? What part of him was real? Both parts? "Tell me why!" he said again, taking a step closer to Morris, his grip on that knife tightening.

"I'll tell you why," Maddy blurted out as tears rolled down her face—tears not of sadness but of emotion that couldn't be controlled. "Because I was a gift. An offering. A testament to the king's power. I was nothing more than a symbol of my mother's submission to your father. The ultimate symbol, and the ultimate submission. A mother handing over her child to please the angry god. Some twisted version of Abraham offering his child to God, the oldest story in both the Old Testament and the Quran." She turned to her father, facing him in a way she hadn't in all the years she'd known him. "Isn't that right, dad? Father? Papa? A gift to save your life? You traded my life for yours, didn't you? I was a just a ransom so you could save your own ass!"

"I saved us both!" Morris shouted, pulling at the ropes that held him to the chair. His neck was straining, his eyes bulging, a vein throbbing on the side of his head. "If I'd tried to do something ridiculous like sue for custody or claim in public that you were my child, what do you think the Sheikh would have done? Smiled and said sure, you fucked my royal wife and knocked her up? No problem. Here's your child. No harm done." He snorted and shook his head. "We'd all be dead now, Maddy. You, me, and your goddamn mother, the psycho who started all of this."

Maddy shook her head as she glanced at that knife again in her peripheral vision. "You left me to a fate worse than death, you cowardly bastard. Your own daughter!"

Morris blinked, a frown crossing his face even as the blood rushed out of it until he was a ghostly white. "You . . . you remember?" His frown deepened, and he shook his head rapidly, almost like he was having a small seizure. But his old eyes were focused and alert, and when he glanced back at Maddy she could see the pain in it. Pain, anger, and confusion. He looked at the Sheikh and then back at his daughter, his body finally relaxing as he exhaled like he was giving up. "Oh, God, Maddy. They told me you wouldn't remember a thing. Neither of you would." He looked at the Sheikh again. "It seemed to work on you. And it seemed to work on her for years. Why isn't it working anymore?"

"What? Spit it out, Morris," said Imraan. "What are you talking about? Some kind of brainwashing? You mentioned hypnosis before. Hypnosis? You had us *hypnotized*so we wouldn't remember?"

Morris clenched his jaw, his eyes glossy with tears. "Oh, God, Maddy. I didn't know what that madwoman would do, what she'd allow him to do to you! And the moment I found out, I did what I could to get you back! To make you forget! Oh, God, I'm so sorry, Maddy."

Maddy didn't say a word. She just looked at her

father, then glanced at her stepbrother. She felt cold inside, a strange calmness drifting through her like a lazy breeze. Did he really think for all these years that she had no memory of what had been done to her? No, the memories weren't available to her, but they were there in primal form, fueling the fire that had sustained her this long. She'd never spoken of it; but then again, they'd never really had many father-daughter chats at the breakfast table, had they. They'd always talked business, and Maddy had never asked him about the snippets of her past that sometimes came to her in nightmares. Why the fuck not? It wasn't like she was afraid of confrontation. Why hadn't she brought it up?

And then it hit her: if she and Imraan had really been hypnotized, maybe the hypnotism worked differently on her. While he'd blocked out the memories completely, the memories had stayed available to her, but locked behind a psychic wall of sorts, creating a split in her mind. So for her it was like those things happened to someone else, even though she knew they'd happened to her. Was that possible? Could it have played out that way?

So what had brought down that wall, brought the memories back into focus, made them *her* memories again? Made them real. Perhaps made *her* real.

A spark of heat cut through the chill that was taking over, and she glanced over at Imraan. The Sheikh stood tall in the center of the room, his face hard, his jaw tight, his green eyes focused like daggers on her father. But then he turned to her as if he could sense what she was thinking, and in that moment she wanted to go to him, tell him she believed him, that she trusted him to protect her, that although she knew he was as damaged and broken as she was, a loose cannon just like she was, she still trusted him with her life, her sanity, her body . . . everything.

That warmth began to take over as she stared into his eyes, and she felt tears rolling down her round cheeks as she nodded absentmindedly and then slowly turned to her father. "I forgive you," she said softly, not sure why she was saying it, not even sure if she believed it. But the words were coming, and she let them. "I forgive you, dad. But I need to understand what happened. We both need to understand what happened. It's time, dad. Tell us. What happened? How did I end up back with you in Atlanta? Why did both the queens commit suicide? How did Imraan end up becoming Sheikh? Who the hell hypnotizes two children into forgetting their childhood?"

Morris took a slow, shuddering breath, looking up at the dark ceiling and then down at the floor as he exhaled. "There was someone else involved. Another man. An American who was in the Middle East around the same time. He was supposedly setting up a consulting business to help American companies work with Middle Eastern governments, but it turned out he was just beginning his career with the CIA. His name was John Benson, and what happened in Wahaad twenty years ago was his first big win. We all made deals back then: I got my daughter back, and Benson became a star in the CIA by getting rid of an oppressive Sheikh and installing his son on the throne."

Imraan frowned, his hand going up to his jaw. He rubbed his dark stubble, grimacing as he began to pace. "So Benson had my father and his two queens killed? Faked my father's accident? Made it look like the Sheikhas killed themselves in a suicide pact? Then he put Maddy and myself through some CIA hypnotism program so we'd forget what happened? And he gets a promotion and we all live happily ever after." He nodded, folding his arms across his broad chest and exhaling. "Perhaps I should begin to torture you to see how much more ridiculous your lies can get, old man."

Morris snorted. "I like that line: We all live happily ever after," he said, ignoring the Sheikh's threat and shaking his head. "You have no idea, Imraan. No goddamn idea."

25

Imraan had no idea if Morris was lying or not. The Sheikh was usually good at reading people, and all signs pointed to Morris telling the truth: steady eye contact, no facial tics, no involuntary tapping of the feet, no clenched fists. His breathing was steady, almost like the man was supremely relaxed, even relieved! Was it possible this story was true? Hypnotism? The CIA?

"Why?" Imraan said. "Why would the CIA even care about the tiny kingdom of Wahaad? We are barely on the map."

Morris shrugged. "It was a different map back then, I guess. Or perhaps they were building the damned map. But hey, I'm a goddamn bookie from the streets of Atlanta, not a political genius. All I know is that this guy Benson was there, and he was working on some kind of deal with your father." He looked at Maddy, his eyes softening for a moment before he glanced down at the floor. "In fact it was Benson who came to me . . ." He hesitated, swallowing hard as his eyes misted up. "Benson came to me with the truth about what was happening, what those sick, twisted people were doing to my daughter. And—"

"Don't pretend like you were any better!" Maddy snarled, taking a step closer as the Sheikh tensed up. He saw the way she had been glancing at the dagger in his hand, and knew he needed to stay alert. This woman was as unpredictable as he was—as unpredictable as all of this was. "You walked away. You left me there! You're worse than they were!"

"I left, but I came back," Morris replied, his eyes still hazy with the mist of tears. "And I would have killed them all if I had the chance. Including your mother. Hell, I would have killed her first!"

Imraan's jaw tightened and he exhaled hard. "So who did kill them? Some unnamed CIA assassins? Where are their bodies? Burned? Buried?"

Morris shook his head, his eyes narrowing as he glanced up at the Sheikh. "Benson was just starting out with the CIA back then. He didn't have the authority or the influence to order hits and cover-ups—

especially not on a Sheikh and his queens! He was a finesses guy, a dealmaker. And he made a deal. With all of us."

"What are you saying?" Imraan said, his breath catching in his throat.

"It's not what I'm saying," Morris whispered, his eyes lighting up for a moment almost like he was enjoying this. "It's what I didn't say. I never said they were dead, Imraan."

The Sheikh blinked as he processed it all, and one look at Maddy told him she was stunned as well. He watched her expression slowly harden, her throat move as she swallowed hard. He could feel what she was feeling, almost like he could read her mind, sense her emotions. She wasn't just shocked. She was exhilarated, thrilled, almost drunk with a sudden feeling of twisted joy.

Because if the old Sheikh and his wives were alive, it meant that they could be killed.

Imraan almost choked as he felt a maddening need for revenge send sparks through his body, and he glanced over at Maddy and saw the way she was looking at him, the corner of her full lips twisted into a smile. Ya Allah, they didn't share any blood, but they shared something deeper, something darker, a common beginning that had turned them into the twisted people they were. She was fantasizing about the same thing he was, wasn't she?

"Where?" said the Sheikh. Just one word. "*Where*?!"

Morris closed his eyes and shook his head. "Somewhere in Europe. Benson never told me. That was the foundation of the deal. He let them move millions of dollars to anonymous Swiss bank accounts and then disappear. A fake plane crash for your father. Suicide for the queens. The orphan son gets the throne. And the daughter . . . well, it was like she never existed. Everyone goes their separate ways. No one talks. No one remembers anything."

"Why?" Maddy said. "Why would this guy do all of that? And how? How could he convince the old Sheikh and his wives to give up their kingdom and go into exile for the rest of their lives? What did he have on them?"

Morris shrugged. "Nobody told me shit. This is all I know." Then he looked up at the Sheikh. "But you can ask your father himself. Maybe Gaurina and Khalifa too, if they're still with him."

"How do I find them?" said the Sheikh.

Morris glanced over at Maddy and then back at the Sheikh. "Who do you think kidnapped her to begin with, Imraan? The old man wants her back. I don't know why, but I can damned well guess. He was a madman then, so there's a helluva good chance he's still a fucking lunatic. He knows you have her, and I doubt he's just going to say to hell with it and give up now."

The Sheikh frowned, turning away from Morris and beginning to pace. What was Morris suggesting? That Imraan use Maddy as bait? Let his father kidnap her once again, this time from the Royal Palace of Wahaad, so they could follow the trail back to Europe or wherever? But Imraan had sworn to protect Maddy. Could he possibly risk losing her just for revenge?

"It's not just revenge," came her voice from behind him, and the moment he turned he knew what he'd see in her eyes: determination, strength, and madness. Pure madness. "It's justice. They don't deserve to live happily ever after, and we'll never be able to live in peace if we don't finish this. This is our story, Imraan. This is our path, and we have to walk it to the end. I'll do it. I'm going to do it. They'll come for me here, and I'm going to let them take me."

"No, Maddy," he said, shaking his head even though his blood was rising along with hers. "The risk is too great. What if I lose the trail?"

"Simple. Don't lose the trail," she said, taking a step towards him, her smile challenging him.

"What if I cannot get you out in time?" the Sheikh said, his own smile coming in strong as he felt her madness infecting him.

"I survived those monsters once. I'll survive them again. Just try not to take twenty years to find me this time, though."

The Sheikh blinked as he looked at his stepsister—

really looked at her. Ya Allah, she is mine, came the thought again. Mine and mine alone. And she is right: this is our story, our journey, our happily ever after. And the path to light sometimes goes through darkness, the journey through peace sometimes winds its way through violence.

Slowly Imraan nodded his head, his mind racing as he wondered how long it would be before his father's men made their way past his palace walls. He'd never worried about security too much: Wahaad was wealthy, peaceful, and mostly crime-free. The Sheikh had stayed away from controversy both within his borders and outside them. There were two armed guards at the front gate, but they were mostly for show. Imraan was almost certain they'd never fired their weapons in all his time as Sheikh. As for security within the Palace . . . ya Allah, it barely existed beyond the smiling attendants, most of whom wouldn't know how to fight their way out of a paper bag!

He blinked as he looked at Maddy again, and then slowly he nodded. "All right," he said softly, his words catching in his throat when he realized that he felt real fear in that moment. She matters, he thought, not sure if he felt panic or joy. By God, she matters!

He took a breath and then turned towards Morris, glancing at his chaffed wrists and bound ankles. "I'll untie you," he said quietly, taking a step towards the seated old man. But just as he got close he felt the movement of air, and he turned just in time to see the door flung open as men with black head-scarves carrying silenced handguns stormed in.

The man leading the charge put two bullets into old man Morris's chest before the Sheikh had a chance to even breathe, and before he could throw a punch he was surrounded and told to get down on his knees.

"*Khadhha. Takhudh ealaa hadin sawa*," said the leader of the invading group, nodding at his men as they grabbed Maddy and tied her wrists as she stared in shock at her father taking his last breath before his head slumped down and he hung limp, still bound to the chair. The masked leader looked back at Imraan and gestured towards the door with his gun. "Your father would like to see both of you at your earliest convenience. This way, please."

26

"**P**lease. Make yourselves comfortable."

The voice sent a chill down Maddy's spine, and she felt every fiber in her body tense up as she forced herself to look upon the man who'd stolen her childhood from her, the man who'd now stolen her father from her . . . the man who was going to die by her hand, if it was the last thing she did.

She sensed Imraan tense up as well as he stood beside her in the sparsely furnished great room of the old French house where they'd been brought. Those armed guards had never left them alone, and their guns had always been drawn, always pointed at both Imraan and Maddy. There had never been a chance at escape during the flight from Wahaad to the private terminal in Paris on an unmarked jet; but then again, escape wasn't the plan.

Imraan stayed quiet beside her, his green eyes unblinking and focused, riveted on his father's wrinkled old face. They shared those green eyes, but almost nothing else, Maddy thought as she glanced at father and son. Perhaps genetics was not destiny after all. She hoped to God it wasn't, because she and Imraan were going to have to trust each other—especially since they'd never had a chance to talk about what they were going to do here.

"We are comfortable," Imraan said coolly, replying for the both of them, taking a step toward his father as every gunman in the room trained his weapon on the young Sheikh. "How do you feel, Father? Comfortable as well?" He glanced around the room. "You certainly look comfortable. It is not the Royal Palace of Wahaad, but it seems spacious. The electricity bill is probably a bit lower, yes?"

The old Sheikh snorted, raising an eyebrow as he glanced at his son. He still had not even looked at Maddy, she realized, and that sent another chill down her spine for some reason.

"Ah, Imraan. You always were quick with the wit," he said, snorting again as he shook his head. "Perhaps that is why your stepmother enjoyed your company so much."

Imraan's jaw tightened, but he didn't flinch. "That is not the reason she enjoyed my company so much," he said without hesitation.

Maddy frowned as she glanced over at Imraan, wondering what game he was playing—if he was playing a game at all. Was he trying to get a rise out of the old Sheikh? Was he trying to stand up to his father? Or was he simply saying what came to his mind, improvising, winging it, finding his way through the darkness of his memories as she stood by his side, both of them facing the monster who'd created them—or at least one of the monsters.

The old Sheikh grunted, his eyes shining dark green as he nodded as if to acknowledge that perhaps his son had grown into a worthy adversary. "So you remember," he said softly. "Good. Perhaps you will get a chance to remind the Begum Gaurina of her youth before this is all over." Then he took a breath, and for the first time he trained his eyes on Maddy. "Just as I will get a chance to remember my own days of youth and power. Yes, my sweet Madeline?" He smiled, showing those all-too-familiar yellowed teeth that made Maddy's blood run cold. "Do you know it was I who named you? And legend has it that naming a thing gives one power over it. Power forever."

"I go by Maddy, not Madeline. And I am not a *thing*," she said, surprised at how steady her voice sounded even though her insides were churning like storm waters. "As for power . . . well, let's see what you got, old man."

She could tell that Imraan turned to her when she spoke, but she kept her eyes trained on the old Sheikh. She wasn't sure what game she was playing either. It was clear what the old man wanted, and it was equally apparent—given the number of armed men in the room—that the end result was going to be a bullet in her head if she tried anything stupid. So her only chance was to get him alone, to see if she could get him to make the mistake of stepping into a room alone with her. Perhaps he still thought of her as that powerless little girl. Maybe he didn't notice that her legs and arms were strong, her back straight and tight, her knuckles bruised and healed over so many times it was impossible to count. Maybe, like so many delusional men, he overestimated his strength and underestimated hers. Maybe, just maybe . . .

"You remember all of it, do you not, sweet Madeline?" he said, the focus of his eyes making her shiver so hard she wasn't certain she could do this. He grinned, glancing at Imraan and then back at her. "I am glad. I wanted that to be part of the deal I made with Benson, but he refused, the soft-hearted fool. I *wanted* you to remember me. All of me. Every inch."

Maddy almost leaped across the room, teeth bared and claws drawn, but the steady gaze of Imraan made her hold her ground. They were a team, she realized, suddenly hyper-aware of her stepbrother looking at her as she fought her feelings, wrestled her memories, did her damned best to stay in the game.

She took a breath and composed herself, tossing her long brown hair over her bruised shoulders and glancing up at the mad old Sheikh. "Well, I barely remember anything. It was so long ago. And so . . . inconsequential." She swallowed hard when she saw the old Sheikh flinch. She'd have to keep pushing. She could break him, she knew. Break him without touching him. Then . . . then she'd get her chance to touch him. Her way, not his. Break him her way, not his. "Not to mention that I've had so much better since then," she said, throwing her head back and smiling, glancing over at Imraan, fluttering her eyelids and looking back at the old Sheikh. "Let's just say that the son has exceeded the father on at least one measure."

She could see the color rush to the old Sheikh's dark face, and she knew she'd gotten to him. If there was any reason and common sense dictating the old Sheikh's actions, they'd been pushed to the background as his anger rose, his wounded pride took over, his delusions of grandeur mixing with his illusions of power, making his ego grasp at the chance to prove himself once again.

Her vision clouded over when she saw him step forward and grab her by the hair, but she stood her ground and held her fists close to her body. She saw the armed guards tense up, one of them call out something in Arabic to the old Sheikh. But the old king was beyond reason, and he shouted at his guards in Arabic as he pulled her towards the back rooms of the old French house.

"No," she whispered, but this time she wasn't talking to the old Sheikh but to his son, to her protector. She'd seen Imraan's face contort in anger, his eyes glaze over with rage. "No," she whispered urgently to him as she let herself be led away from the group.

Maddy glanced at the armed guards and then back at Imraan, trying to tell him with her eyes that he needed to do his part. He needed to get out of that room as well, away from the sights of ten men with guns. She couldn't do a thing to the old Sheikh knowing that Imraan was at the mercy of his guards! Oh, God, would he understand? Would he understand what he needed to do while she was doing what *she* needed to do?!

And just as she was pulled out of sight of Imraan, she saw his face go calm, his eyes narrow, his jaw tighten. There was the slightest nod in his head, and a long, slow blink as if to say good luck, God bless, and I love you.

Then she heard his voice just as he disappeared from view:

"Where are you?" came Imraan's voice, loud and clear. "Where are you, Gaurina? Where are you, my beautiful stepmother?"

27

She stepped out from behind a curtain as if it had been planned, as if this were all a stage and she was the lead actress. She'd aged, but her presence still made Imraan's breath catch as those memories of her emerged so strong he found it hard to breathe.

He blinked as images of her naked breasts came rushing to him, her dark red nipples pushed into his teenage face as she stroked his young, hard cock. Ya Allah, he thought as he felt himself stiffen even at the sight of her now, twenty years later. I am beyond repair, am I not? I hate her but I want her! I love the daughter but I still want to push my cock into the mother! What special kind of hell will I burn in when it is my time?! The same hell my father is destined for?!

Genetics is not destiny, he told himself as he swallowed hard, watching the woman who'd taken his innocence step into the fading light of the grand old room. She wore a long dark tunic, traditional Arab dress but with no head covering. Her hair was still thick and lustrous, that mix of Arabian and European blood giving her skin a light brown sheen that had been passed on to Maddy.

Genetics is not destiny, he told himself again as he watched her walk towards him like a dream or perhaps a nightmare. But that does not mean destiny does not exist. It does, and Maddy is my destiny.

He fought the urge to try to go after Maddy, pushing aside the thought of what might be going on behind closed doors. Clearly Maddy had wanted to get his father to lose his temper and pull her away from the guards. But did she want more than that? Was it possible her memories of that time were not all horror and pain?

Ya Allah, what are you thinking, the Sheikh told himself as his head spun from the way his stepmother was looking at him, her light brown eyes catching the light and reflecting it like she was hypnotizing him. He blinked again, wondering what was happening to him. Was it the impact of seeing her again? This woman who'd had such an impact on him when he was a child? Or was it something else, something more?

He saw her lips move, but he couldn't hear what she was saying. He stepped closer, frowning as he tried to make out the words, and just as his eyes locked in

on hers, one searing memory emerged from the recesses of his mind, cutting so hard he almost crumpled to the floor.

"Ya Allah, you goddamn witch," he muttered as he
watched her whisper and stare at him. "It was you!
You were the hypnotist. Benson was here because he
was trying to recruit you to work for the CIA! Now I
remember you telling me that. You told me all of it .
. . right before you made me forget it! He thought he
could use you for interrogations, to plan operations,
even to help with PTSD for his agents!"

Gaurina paused, her eyelids fluttering as if she was
surprised that he remembered. Her hesitation was
enough, and the Sheikh shook his head to clear it,
and now he knew he was in control of himself again.
She wasn't getting into his head. Never again.

But perhaps she will believe she can get into my
head again, he told himself. That is what my stepsister
is doing right now with my father, is she not? These
people have lived in exile for two decades, closed off
from reality, living in a world of memories . . . memories of a time when they yielded absolute power over
their worlds, their children, the two of us. Perhaps
they still believe we are children, and perhaps that is
our way through this.

And so the Sheikh swallowed hard and blinked, trying to look confused as he stared into his stepmother's brown eyes. He took another step towards her,

ignoring the fact that his body was reacting to hers in a way he didn't want to be true. This would not be easy, but it was the only way. He needed to get her alone, away from the guards.

But then what, he wondered as he watched her begin to mutter something under her breath again, her alluring eyes regaining that calm confidence that had pulled him under her power once before. Then what?

28

I can kill him, but then what? Maddy thought as she heard the old Sheikh wheeze from the strain of dragging her into the large room and kicking the door shut. She could smell his sweat, and it reminded her of things she couldn't forget. She was scared, but excited at the same time. In a way she'd fantasized about having this chance, hadn't she? She'd never imagined it could happen, but now here she was, with a chance to exorcise her demons!

So why am I hesitating, she wondered as she watched him take deep breaths as he stood above her. Why am I on the floor, sitting on my ass when the man who twisted me into the person I am is right here for the taking? Is it just common sense, knowing that there are armed men outside the door? Or is it because I'm scared to exorcise those demons? Scared to purge those memories? Scared to let go of the darkness that made me who I am, forms the core of my being? Or am I just scared? Just straight up fucking scared, like a goddamn child?!

And now she'd done it, opened the door to fear. She could feel it creep in, the chill running through her as she sat frozen and watched the old Sheikh undo his tunic.

"You say you remember it all," he whispered as he smiled down at her. "But I assure you, my sweet Madeline, it will be more than you remember. Much more. Come now, spread for me just like you used to. Spread for me like a good girl."

"She was never a good girl," came a woman's voice, and Maddy frowned as she stared in the direction of the new presence. The woman was behind the old Sheikh, and Maddy couldn't see her clearly. The voice was familiar, though, and Maddy felt that chill change form as she listened. "None of us were good girls, great Sheikh. But you knew that, did you not? You always knew that. You also know that it was a long time ago. We are not the people we were twenty years ago. Our time has passed, Sheikh. It is time to make way for the next generation, the next cycle. It is time."

The Sheikh's mouth opened wide, his eyes rolling up in his head in a way that made Maddy's toes curl. She watched in shock as he gasped slowly, a sick, gurgling noise coming as blood poured from his gaping mouth. He staggered forward, going down on his knees before her, and it was only when he fell face-forward, his head landing right between Maddy's spread legs, did she see the jeweled hilt of the dagger sticking out from between his shoulder blades.

"Oh, shit," Maddy muttered, staring down as the old Sheikh took his last breath, his blood flowing around her spread legs just like her blood had flowed from his touch once. She looked up at the woman, and only when she looked into her eyes did she know who it was. "Khalifa," she whispered as the shock rocked her body so hard she began to shiver. She'd seen blood before, drawn it herself. But this was different. This was . . . family. "Oh, shit, Khalifa."

"Stay quiet," the old queen said, glancing at the door and then back at her. "We are safe so long as this door stays closed. The guards will not dare disturb the Sheikh unless he calls for them."

Maddy backed away from the old Sheikh's body, her senses coming back as she evaluated the situation. She glanced at Khalifa, looking into the old queen's eyes. It was her, no doubt. The first Sheikha. Imraan's mother. The woman who'd watched from the shadows as her own husband had done what he did, while her sister-wife had held her own daughter down.

You can't trust her, Maddy told herself, thinking
of that dagger sticking out of the dead Sheikh's back.
The jeweled hilt matched the one she'd seen Imraan
carrying, and that bothered her in a way she couldn't
understand. Still, right now she needed to decide how
to handle Khalifa.

Time stood still for Maddy as she looked into the
Sheikha's eyes. They were sand-colored and focused,
a strange energy radiating from them even though
her face was wrinkled and worn. Those eyes had seen
a lot, hadn't they? And yet there was a light in them.
Why?

"Why?" Maddy said, glancing at the dead Sheikh
and then back up at her stepmother.

"The question shouldn't be just why—it should be
why now? Why not twenty years ago when it would
have made a difference?" Khalifa shrugged, looking
at her dead husband and then back at Maddy. "And
I do not know the answer to that. Or perhaps I do
not want to face the answer: that I was a coward. I
was content to stand in the shadows and let all of
this happen."

Maddy tightened as she watched the Sheikha's eyes.
Something didn't smell right here. She remembered
Khalifa watching from those shadows . . . *watching*.
The first Sheikha hadn't been content to hide in her
room like a coward. She'd stood there and watched,
and that was as bad as Gaurina holding her down
while the Sheikh took her innocence, her childhood,

and her sanity all at once. Nope. This wasn't going to be as easy as Maddy nodding her head and saying all was forgiven. You're gonna die too, you scheming bitch. At least my mother accepted her insanity, embraced her crazy, understood that she was a monster. This woman wanted to believe she wasn't as bad as the others. Fuck her. Fuck them all.

Maddy wanted to say all this, and she almost did. A part of her wanted to say fuck it, perhaps this was where it all ended. Who cared if she got gunned down by those men outside. But then she realized she wanted to live, and she wanted it more than anything. Imraan was facing his own demons in another room in this dark old house, and he was going to need her. He was going to need her today, tomorrow, and forever. She was going to live, and so she'd need to shut the hell up and play along.

"What now?" she said, nodding at Khalifa, knowing she'd have to match her wits against this old queen even though she could easily overpower her. "Can you talk to your men outside? Get them to leave?"

Khalifa shook her head. "They are not my men. They answer to the Sheikh, and him alone. But so long as we stay in here, they will not dare enter."

Maddy looked around. There was a window at the far end of the room. "What about that? Does it lead outside?"

"It leads to an enclosed courtyard. But the courtyard will be empty, and perhaps you can enter through another window and get to the far side of the house. There will be no one there. You should be able to find your way out. If you want."

Maddy cocked her head and frowned. "If I want?" she said slowly. "Why would I *not*want to get the hell out of here?"

"You came here for a reason, did you not?"

"I was kidnapped and brought here. Kidnapped three separate times, by the way."

"Fate sometimes takes a twisted path to get you to your destiny."

Maddy snorted. "Oh, please! You're going to blame fate and destiny instead of taking responsibility for the choices all of you made?" She glanced at the dagger, its jeweled handle shining in the dim light, the hilt sticking straight out of the Sheikh's back like Excalibur in the stone. "I should just—"

"Do it," Khalifa whispered, the words coming so quick it startled Maddy. "Take it out of him. Slit my throat—Allah knows I deserve it! Then go fulfill your destiny. Fulfill *all*our destinies!"

Maddy blinked as she tried to figure out what game the old woman was playing. "What destiny? What the hell are you talking about, you crazy old—"

"Kill her!" Khalifa whispered, her eyes going wide and then narrowing again. "You have to do it before my son does it. Kill your mother before Imraan does it!"

"What?" Maddy said, her head spinning as she tried

to make sense of what Khalifa was saying. "What . . . why . . ."

"He is going to kill her. Not for what she did to him, but for what she did to you. And if he does that, he will be broken beyond repair. The conflict will consume him, weaken him just like it did his father. It has to be you who does it. Then you can make Imraan into the man his father once was. Resolve his conflict by killing her yourself."

"I don't understand. What conflict?"

Khalifa took a breath, her eyes focusing on Maddy's. "He was a boy when she seduced him. What effect do you think it had on him, when he was going through his own sexual awakening?"

Maddy went pale as her thoughts raced, her body shuddered, her vision blurred. A strapping teenage boy seduced by his alluring stepmother? Yes, he was a victim. Yes, he was manipulated. But the psychological experience was not the same as it was for her with the old Sheikh. While Maddy was held down, physically overwhelmed and overpowered, Imraan must have known that he was physically in control at all times. Yes, the mental hold she had on him had its own power, its own influence, but for Imraan there was at least the illusion of choice.

Oh, God, Maddy thought as she read Khalifa's expression. Imraan believes he *chose* to have sex with his stepmother, even though she manipulated him into it, controlled his body with her touch and her words. And so perhaps . . . perhaps he believes he loved her? That he still loves her? Is that the conflict she's talking about? Oh, God, is the "other woman" in my twisted love story my own fucking mother?!

And as if a door had burst open somewhere at the back of her psyche, Maddy felt a flood of emotions roll in like a tidal wave, the twin horses of doubt and jealousy leading the charge. She stared at Khalifa, wondering who was manipulating whom in that moment, who was telling the truth, who was lying, who was insane, and who wasn't.

We're all insane, came the thought as she pictured her stepbrother naked and glistening, pushing himself into her mother as she screamed in ecstasy. Yes, we're all insane, all twisted, all damaged beyond repair. There's no way out, is there? No way out.

Through the madness she saw a glint of silver steel, a flash of red ruby, a glimmer of green emerald. The knife, part of an old set. One belonged to Imraan, and the other, Maddy realized, belonged to her.

29

"I belong to you," Gaurina whispered, touching his neck and standing so close he could feel her breasts against his chest. "I always have, Imraan. Do you remember?"

Imraan took a long breath as he felt his cock swell, his eyes glazing over with arousal. But it was a sickening arousal, not like what he'd felt with Maddy. He almost choked when he realized what he was thinking, that he was unconsciously comparing the mother with the daughter. What kind of twisted creature was he? Was he born this way, or did this woman standing up against him turn him into the monster he was?

It would be so easy to finish this, he thought as he watched her undo the top of her robe. He glanced at her neck, thin and delicate. He could end this so easily. He wouldn't even need to use both hands. He was in control, he told himself. In total control.

Then why am I frozen, shivering like a scared child, aroused and repelled at the same time, hatred and desire moving through me together like two lovers dancing? Why do I want to kill her one moment, fuck her the next, just like I did with Maddy? Which one of us is the monster?

We are all monsters, came the response from somewhere inside him, and he felt his face twist into a smile as he reached out and grasped Gaurina by the back of her neck, pulling her close and leaning in until he could feel her breath against his lips. All of us. We were born that way, and either you can fight it or embrace it. You fucked this woman a hundred times as a teenager. You were always taller than her, heavier than her, stronger than her. You could have snapped her like a twig, ended it any time you wanted, yes? But instead you let her stroke you until you were hard like a rock, you pushed your face between her legs when she asked you to lick her, you slid your cock into her rear when she begged you to stretch her wide and take her deep.

And then, he told himself as he felt her fingers

reach down between his legs and find his hardness, when she asked you if you loved her, what did you say? What did you say, Imraan? Do you remember?

"I don't want to remember," he muttered, pushing her hand away, grasping her by the throat as he felt a rage he'd never experienced rise up so fast he almost gagged even as he tried to hold back from choking the life out of Gaurina. "I cannot trust you, and I cannot trust my memories."

"I agree," Gaurina whispered, her face turning red as Imraan began to squeeze her throat. "Then trust what you've always trusted, Imraan. Your body. What does your body want? Answer me, Imraan. What does your body want?"

"To kill you," the Sheikh answered, pressing harder on her throat even as he felt his cock stiffen along with his grip. Already he could feel her breathing getting labored, her body tensing up. A little more pressure and it would be done. He would be . . . free? Or would he be trapped forever, something in the back of his mind always whispering that he'd killed the woman he once . . . loved?

Suddenly the Sheikh let go of her throat, stepping away from Gaurina as she fell to the floor, taking huge gulps of air even as she stared up at him and smiled.

"You loved me," she whispered as she massaged her throat. Slowly she rose to her knees and beckoned to the Sheikh with her head. "You said it so many times,

Imraan. Say it again. Say it again while I remind you what your body wants."

Gaurina moved forward on her knees, licking her lips as the Sheikh felt his cock push against the fabric of his trousers. Images were passing through his mind so fast he was dizzy: memories of her breasts, her lips, her vagina—all of them so powerful, all of them burned in his psyche so deep he knew there was no escape.

So just give in, he thought as he felt her unzip him and bring her mouth close. Just give in. If you are a monster, then embrace it like everyone else in your family has done. Perhaps genetics is destiny, and if there is not a thread of goodness in your line, then do not fight the darkness because you *are* the darkness.

You, your stepsister, your stepmother, your father . . .

. . . and your mother.

30

"**I** am his mother," Khalifa said as Maddy drew the knife from the old Sheikh's back and wiped it off on the dead man's tunic. "But I am also *your* mother in a way."

"Stepmother," Maddy said, her voice strong as she felt a soothing confidence flow through her as she gripped the knife. It felt good in her hand. Cold, sharp, and clear. Exactly what she needed right now.

Khalifa shook her head. "We did not distinguish at the time. We were all one family."

Maddy snorted as she stood. "A family where everyone fucked everyone else. Forgive me if I don't call you mommy."

Khalifa glanced at the knife, a smile slowly emerging. "Do you not want to know about your family before we are all gone?"

"I know enough to know that I want you all gone as soon as fucking possible," Maddy muttered, taking a step as she tightened her grip on the knife.

"And then what? You and my son will go on with your lives as if nothing happened, still believing that you are the spawn of monsters? Acting out the patterns of your parents in your private lives, your relationships, with your own children?"

"What do you care?" Maddy said stubbornly. "And anyway, we *are* the spawn of monsters, you being one of those monsters that created the two of us, turned us into what we are." She glanced at the knife again, frowning as she wondered what came next. She wanted to end this, finish Khalifa, crawl out that window and find Gaurina and slit her damned throat. But something about Khalifa's tone made her hesitate. This woman was calm, as if she was resigned to her fate, had decided that she wanted to end this too. Perhaps she had something of value to say before she died.

"All right," Maddy said finally, even though she could feel her hand shake. "Any last words?"

Khalifa took a breath and slowly sat on a leather divan up against the faded red walls of the old French house. "You have not asked the question, but I will answer it anyway. I will tell you about her, about all of us, about the promises we made, the promises we broke. But it starts with her. Your mother."

Maddy's hand was trembling so much it scared her, and she lowered the knife and closed her eyes as she felt those tears that came from somewhere deep inside roll down her cheeks. She nodded, slowly going down on her haunches and nodding again. "Go on," she said quietly. "Go on."

"She was wild, out of control, insane. But she was also special, brilliant, and strong in a way that captivated everyone who came into contact with her. Everyone fell in love with her. Everyone was scared of her. Everyone bowed to her—if not in public, then certainly behind closed doors. The Sheikh, myself, your stepbrother, your father . . . even Benson."

"The CIA agent?" Maddy snorted and rolled her eyes. "He fucked her too? How shocking. Excuse me if I don't gasp in surprise."

Khalifa smiled and shook her head. "He never wanted her for a lover. He wanted to recruit her. In fact, he still does. She is the reason we are all still alive!" She raised an eyebrow as she glanced at her dead husband. "Well, most of us, at least."

"Why? What the hell does the CIA want with my mother?"

Khalifa laughed. "Look into her eyes and you will see. But do not stare too long."

Maddy frowned as she tried to make sense of Khalifa's cryptic remarks. She tried to think back, but the memories of her mother were inextricably mixed with those of the old Sheikh, those moments of darkness and fear, panic and pain. She searched herself for a clear memory of her mother's eyes, but it would not come. And so Maddy knew she'd have to go . . . go to her mother.

31

They crawled out the window, crept through the courtyard, Khalifa leading the way as Maddy followed, knife in hand, wondering what the hell she was doing. Was Khalifa leading her into a trap? What kind of trap? If Khalifa wanted her dead, all she'd have had to do would have been to scream and call the dead Sheikh's guards into the room. As for why she'd killed her husband . . . who the hell knew that either! Remorse? Guilt? After twenty years of living the good life in Paris?! What was driving this old queen?

Something Khalifa had said came back to Maddy as they stopped on the far side of the courtyard, outside a darkened window. What had she said about Gaurina? That everyone loved her, everyone wanted her, everyone bowed to her? So was it jealousy then? As simple as that? After all, back then Khalifa would have been the odd one out, right? The old Sheikh had his prize in Maddy, and everyone else was fucking Gaurina! Was Khalifa just straight-up jealous? Was she in love with Gaurina too? Was this more twisted than anyone could imagine? Who the hell knew.

Keep your head straight and don't lose your nerve, Maddy told herself as she gripped the knife and tested the window to the empty room on the far side of the courtyard. It was open, and she pulled herself up and then helped Khalifa enter. It smelled musty but clean, and Khalifa hurried to the door and put her ear to it, waiting for a moment before beckoning to Maddy.

"Come. There is no one. Come."

They entered the dark, empty hallways of the mansion, and Maddy followed the old queen, the two of them keeping to the walls until they could see the lights of the great room in the distance, around a corner. Khalifa listened at another door and nodded.

"They are in here. The guards will stay outside the other room because their Sheikh is in there," she whispered. "We can enter."

Maddy tightened when she saw the old queen's eyes. She didn't trust this woman. Khalifa had been there at the worst of times, watching from the wings, perhaps even directing the show. Sure, Maddy couldn't trust her own memories either, and so she had to trust the only thing that she knew for a fact was real: Her body, her gut, her damned instincts.

So she shook her head and stepped close to the queen, holding the shining double-edged blade to her wrinkled throat and gesturing towards the door with her head. "Royalty first, your highness. Come on, you old bitch. Open the door. Slowly now."

They entered the room, and Maddy gasped when she looked at the woman kneeling on the floor in front of her stepbrother. And then suddenly she remembered those eyes, those light brown eyes that seemed to change color if you stared too long at them. Those eyes that were staring into Imraan's, who was sitting cross-legged in front of Gaurina, helpless like a child as he stared back at his stepmother, his first love.

32

"I was your first love, was I not?" she'd whispered as her gaze met his, her voice sounding familiar and soothing, like an ancient lullaby.

"Yes," he'd said, hearing his own voice come out of him like it was someone else speaking. He knew what she was doing, but he couldn't seem to stop her. Perhaps he was already hypnotized. But how? He'd barely looked into her eyes. He'd been on his guard. How could he be at her mercy already, already under her spell?

Unless he'd never broken that spell.

Those words she'd been muttering when she first saw him, the Sheikh thought as he glanced down at his hands, which felt useless and clumsy suddenly.

He'd had them on Gaurina's throat, but he couldn't seem to lift them now. They were dead weight.

Those words, he thought again. Wasn't it true that hypnotists could plant trigger words in their subjects' minds, words that would immediately bring them back under hypnosis, even years after the initiating sessions? Perhaps even twenty years later? Was that what was happening here? Could it happen even though he was vaguely conscious of it happening?

Imraan sensed movement at his left, and he was conscious of the door opening, but he could not turn his head. He was fixed on Gaurina, and it was only when she turned her head that he felt a moment of release. It was not complete release though, and although he was able to turn to glance at the two women who'd just entered the room, he still could not move from his cross-legged position on the floor.

He recognized both the women, but in a distant, twice-removed from reality sort of way. It was like a dream, he thought as he watched Gaurina rise quickly and utter a few words to the younger woman who was holding a dagger to the other woman's throat.

The younger woman's eyelids fluttered, and she lowered the knife immediately. The Sheikh watched in silent awe as the woman he now recognized as his stepsister went down on her knees and then sat cross-legged beside him, as if they were two children obeying their teacher.

She is our teacher, Imraan thought as he watched Gaurina say a few more words in Arabic to Maddy before glancing at Khalifa and nodding, faint smiles on both the old women's lips.

"Do you remember your mother?" Gaurina said, that faint smile still on her lips as she looked at Maddy, then Imraan, finally at Khalifa.

Imraan frowned as he glanced at the familiar face of the older woman who'd just entered. He nodded, realizing that Maddy was nodding too. They'd both been asked the same question, and they were both answering.

"Yes," he heard himself say as he stared into Khalifa's eyes.

"Yes," he heard Maddy say as she looked upon Gaurina's face.

"Good," said Gaurina. "Then we can begin."

"Begin what?" said the Sheikh, glancing down at his hands and wondering why he couldn't raise them to Gaurina's throat once again.

"Begin your new lives," said Khalifa.

"As a family," said Gaurina.

"A happy family," said Khalifa.

"Like we once were. All of us," said Gaurina.

"But first we need to complete the cycle before you are ready to begin the next cycle, the next generation, continue the bloodline," said Khalifa. "Remind both of you what it means to be part of this family."

"Yes," said Gaurina, nodding at Imraan. "Take her clothes off, Imraan."

"What?" said Imraan.

"My daughter. Your sister. Take her clothes off. Now. *Astamae li*," said Gaurina, staring directly into his eyes as she said it.

The Sheikh blinked in confusion when he realized he was moving, that his hands were already pulling off Maddy's dark blue top. He gasped when he felt himself stiffen to full mast again, and a moment later he'd unclasped Maddy's bra, his cock straining for release when he saw her heavy breasts come into view, the smooth, light brown skin of her globes, the dark nipples that were perking up as he watched his own fingers pinch and pull at them.

"She was our gift to your father," Khalifa whispered, drawing close to Gaurina until both queens were sitting flush up against one another, watching their children strip naked. "Now she is your prize. Take her like your father took her. Take her to the place where your father took her. Then you will see what he saw. You will be what he was. All powerful. In control. Head of the family."

"No," groaned the Sheikh, but Gaurina was whispering in Arabic, and his body seemed to be in her control. Soon he was sucking on Maddy's nipples, and although she writhed under his touch, she sat there crosslegged and obedient, without any resistance, her eyes closed, her mouth half open.

"Take off her pants," whispered Gaurina, nodding at Khalifa as the two queens moved towards Maddy, grabbing her bare arms and pulling her down to the wooden floor of the empty room until she lay flat on her back. "Her pants, and her underwear. Strip her bare for all of us to see. Come now. It is all right. Give in. You want her. You have already had her, have you not? Come on. We are all family here."

"I do not want any part of this family," muttered the Sheikh through gritted teeth, trying to control himself but getting that sense of being paralyzed, like in those dreams where you know you are alive and have a body but can't control your movements. "Neither is she. We are going to rid ourselves of the two of you. Now, and forever."

"*Astamae li*," whispered Gaurina, running her fingernails down Maddy's bare neck, down past the curve of her breast, circling her belly-button, that spot where she'd been joined to her mother when she emerged from the womb, untouched and innocent. "Undress her. Do this for us, and I swear you will be released. I will remove the trigger words I planted in both your minds when you were children. I will give you back all your memories, while at the same time freeing you from your pasts. Give yourselves to us, one last time."

"Why?" the Sheikh said, his voice trembling as he watched Gaurina hold his hand and place it on Maddy's crotch until he was stroking her through her black jeans as Khalifa held Maddy's arms down against the floor. "What is wrong with you two? What is wrong with . . . with all of us? Why? *Why*?"

Gaurina laughed, reaching out and patting the monstrous bulge at the seam of Imraan's trousers. "Why?" She glanced back at Khalifa and shrugged. "He asks why," she said like she was mocking the Sheikh. "At least his father understood why he did what he did, why we all did what we did, why we all *enjoyed* what we did. Every moment of it. Every one of us." Gaurina looked at the Sheikh and then back at Khalifa. "Every one of us," she said again.

Khalifa nodded as if in agreement, stroking Maddy's bare arms as the Sheikh looked into his mother's eyes in horror. Then Khalifa looked down at Maddy's bare breasts and up at her son. "We all enjoyed it. You, I, your stepmother. And your stepsister. Yes, even her."

The Sheikh almost doubled over as the sickness rose up so quick his vision blurred. But still he was powerless to reach out and choke the life from these women. "You lie," he managed to say through his constricted breaths. "She was a child. So was I, but at least I was older. At least I could have fought back, stopped it if I . . . if I . . ."

"If you . . . what? If you wanted? Stopped it if you *wanted*?" Khalifa said. "So now you said it yourself! You did not want to stop it, did you? None of it. Because you enjoyed it, just like your sister did. Just like she will enjoy it when you remind her of that time."

"She did not enjoy it. You are lying, and with Allah as my witness I will rip your tongues from your wrinkled throats so your voices are never heard on His earth again."

"You think we are lying?" Gaurina said, raising an eyebrow as she looked down at her half-naked daughter. "Then take her back there and see for yourself. Prove to yourself that she is lying. Take her back there, and let us all see the truth."

"Yes, son. Take her back there. Take us all back there. Then you will see that truth and destiny are one and the same, just like blood and destiny are one and the same. Blood . . . the blood that runs in your veins, pumps through her body, twists through our wrinkled frames. One and the same."

And then the Sheikh suddenly knew the answer to the question of why: Their blood was the answer. They did what they did because it was in their blood. Like the old fable of the scorpion and the snake, the scorpion stings because that is its nature. That is its essence. That is what it was born to do, and it cannot do otherwise, no matter what the consequences. Genetics was indeed destiny, and there was no escaping it.

And if there is no escaping it, the Sheikh thought

as he looked into his mother's eyes and nodded, then I might as well embrace it.

33

Embrace it, Maddy told herself as she glanced up at the two women staring down at her, the Sheikh above her. Embrace what you're feeling, because this is who you are, this is who they are. This is your family, and there's no escaping it.

She'd been listening to them speak, watching them negotiate over her half-stripped body. She'd heard it before, she was certain of it. Two women and their man talking as she was undressed and held down, touched all over. They'd told her she was a woman and a queen, a whore and a slut, a witch and a wife, all at once.

"What?" Maddy said, surprised that she was able to

speak, blinking in confusion when she realized that she'd been dumbstruck as if someone had taken control of her speech and actions all this while. "What's happening? Imraan?"

"Silence," he said, and she frowned when she looked into his twisted face, his narrowed eyes . . . eyes that seemed a darker green than before. He'd always been dominant and authoritative with her, but even in that first meeting, when she was locked in a cage, tied to metal bars and being spanked, she felt safe with him. Now, however . . .

"*Alaistimae waltaen*," she heard Gaurina whisper from above her, and when she tried to move her arms she felt their hands holding her down.

What the fuck is she doing to me, Maddy thought, trying to call Imraan's name again. But the words wouldn't come, and Maddy realized Gaurina was using trigger words, like she'd seen a hypnotist use at a show back in Atlanta. She blinked up at the faces of the old queens again as she felt the Sheikh undo her jeans and pull them off past her wide hips. Then her panties were off, and she stared up in frozen shock as the Sheikh handed the underwear to her own mother.

"See how wet your daughter is for me, Gaurina," the Sheikh growled above her, and Maddy gasped when she felt the air swirl around her naked crotch. She realized that she was indeed wet, aroused beyond belief, and it made her sick to think that perhaps she'd been aroused all that time ago, that first time, the second time, every time!

"No," she muttered, trying to pull her arms free, but the two queens were using their full weight as they held her by the wrists. "No."

"You do not say no to your king, child," Gaurina said. "You do not say no to your father."

"He's not . . . he's not . . ." Maddy stammered, wondering why her words were coming out slurred like she was drunk. She heard Gaurina mutter something else in Arabic, and she felt her tongue go stiff in her mouth, like it was a piece of stone, useless and hard.

She tried to break free again, but all she could do was move her fingers. The strength in her arms seemed beyond her reach, as if it had been locked away. Was this the hypnotism Khalifa had mentioned, that Benson wanted to harness for the CIA? Was Gaurina doing this to her? Or was it Maddy's own fear?

The Sheikh's face was between her legs as her mind raced, and she heard herself moan as she felt his tongue slide into her and curl up like a snake. She could hear the queens laughing as they watched their children play, one child's tongue inside the other, brother and sister, father and daughter, scorpion and snake.

"Do you remember how it felt the first time?" Gaurina whispered as Maddy watched the Sheikh pull his tongue out of her and go up on his knees. He ripped off his tunic, exposing his rock-hard chest and muscled torso. His abdomen was ridged muscle, taut and gleaming, and the peak at the front of his trousers was so large Maddy felt herself being stretched before he even entered her.

Maddy sensed movement above her, and she realized that Khalifa had let go of her arm and had moved away from the scene. Maddy frowned as she watched the old queen cross the room and stand in the corner, half-hidden in the shadows, as if she wanted to distance herself from the scene that was about to unfold. Was she too ladylike and proper to stand near her son when he stripped naked? How nice to be able to fool yourself into believing you're not as twisted as the others in your family. I'll kill you last, you sick bitch.

I have one free hand now, Maddy realized suddenly, and although she couldn't speak clearly, it seemed she could move all right. So she whipped her free arm out, reached for her mother, and grabbed her by the throat, looking up over her head and seeing Gaurina's eyes go wide in shock. The old queen had been distracted, her eyes focused on Imraan undressing, her mind perhaps reliving memories of her own youth, reveling in the sickness of her own past.

Maddy stared up into her mother's eyes as her own mind swirled with thoughts that seemed to have no basis in anything. Was my mother herself abused as a child? Did someone else turn her into the creature she became? Am I just the continuation of the classic cycle of abuse? Was she just an oppressed woman doing what her king and husband demanded?

She saw Gaurina's lips move as if she was trying to whisper something, but Maddy took a breath and squeezed as hard as she could, forcing the trigger words to stick in Gaurina's throat. Maddy watched as her mother's face went red, her eyes widening, pupils dilating, capillaries bursting as the oxygen drained from her body.

Gaurina clawed at Maddy's arm, but the daughter was too strong. Then Gaurina's eyes moved to her sister-queen, Khalifa, who was standing in the shadows and silently watching, not looking away but not stepping in either. Khalifa just shook her head and smiled, and Maddy felt herself smile too even as tears rolled down her face. She could feel a dark energy pour through her as she realized what was happening, what she was doing.

"Tell me you are a victim too," Maddy whispered through her own sobs as she squeezed the life out of her mother. "That there was a reason for what you did, an excuse, an explanation."

But Gaurina's eyes were rolling up in her head, her lips turning blue as she desperately clawed at Maddy's viselike grip. Maddy eased the pressure a bit, hoping Gaurina would look at her and say yes, I was a victim too, just like you were. I was a product of my own past, a creation of others. But there was no response, and Maddy knew there wouldn't be a response. The only words that would come from Gaurina's lips would be those trigger words that had been designed to control, to contain, to constrict.

Still, Maddy eased up just a little more, until a hint of color appeared in the dying queen's lips. Then those lips moved.

"*Alaistimae waltaen*," Gaurina managed to say, and she looked past Maddy and towards the Sheikh, who'd been on his knees as if frozen. "*Alaistimae waltaen!*"

Maddy realized she'd made a mistake, and she gritted her teeth and squeezed again. She cried as she did it, but she cried for herself, not her mother. She cried for herself, because she realized that Gaurina was who she was because it was her essence, it was what was inside her, it was in her blood. And that meant it was in Maddy's blood too, it was part of her too, it was perhaps all of her. There was no excuse, no explanation, no escape.

Then suddenly she felt strong hands close around her own throat, and her eyes went wide when she saw it was Imraan, his eyes glazed over. Maddy was still on her back, reaching up behind her head and strangling her mother as her stepbrother looked down on her and squeezed her windpipe until her eyes felt like they were going to pop out of her head.

I'm going to die, Maddy thought. He's going to kill

me, and then he's going to fuck my mother and live happily ever after. She almost laughed as the insanity of that scenario registered in her suffocating brain, and she looked up at the Sheikh and smiled. You have no excuse either, do you? You've understood that we are what we are because of our blood, not our choices or the choices of others. There's no hope for us. Hypnotism, trigger-words, the cycle of abuse . . . all those excuses are meaningless. We are what we are, and that's the end of the story.

But whose story is ending here, Maddy thought as she looked at her hypnotized brother and then her dying mother. Don't I get to choose that? Perhaps I can't change the ending itself, but I can decide whose story ends first, can't I? And doesn't that change things? Doesn't that mean genetics and destiny might not be the same? Who knows? Who the hell knows!

She looked at Imraan one last time, and then she knew. It was their story, her story, his story. She thought of the two of them playing in that desert spring like newborn babes, when a few days before that she'd been in a cage, at his mercy, being tamed as if she were a wild animal. She thought of the madness with which he'd taken her that first time, the way they'd collapsed against each other, sobbing in confusion, both of them understanding that there was no one else in the world who could ever see them for what they were and still love them.

If that's who I am, then I'm going to embrace it,

love it, use it to get the ending I want, Maddy decided. So she squeezed her mother's throat, using the
last of her own strength and sanity to try and drive
the remaining life out of Gaurina even as she felt
her own vision narrow down to a dark tunnel as the
Sheikh pressed harder.

"It has to be you who does it, who kills Gaurina,"
Khalifa had told her earlier. "If my son does it, the
darkness will own him just like it did his father."

But what will happen to me if I kill my mother,
Maddy wondered. Will I become her? Overtaken by
the darkness that runs in my bloodline? Is that what
Khalifa wants? Is that what *both* the queens want?

And as her vision went black, Maddy understood.
She understood why Khalifa had killed the old Sheikh,
why Khalifa was standing back and watching as Maddy squeezed the life out of Gaurina, why Khalifa had
welcomed her own death by Maddy's hand. This
was their plan. This was the ending they wanted.
They wanted what any parents wanted, what all of
life itself wanted: to replicate, to evolve, to produce
the next generation. They just wanted to make sure
their children understood who they were first, who
they *all* were, what kind of family this was.

Which means if I kill my mother, I will give them
the ending they want, Maddy realized. The moment
she dies, Imraan will be released from his spell. And
then the cycle will be complete. I will become my

mother, I will turn Imraan into his father, and . . . and then what? Will we have children? What of them? What hope will they have?

No, she thought, releasing her mother. I'd rather die than continue this bloodline. This is what the queens wanted, didn't they? The oldest drive in existence, the need to see your line go on. Genetics, destiny, and simple biology . . . all of it mixed with the madness that defined these people's lives. No. It won't happen.

You won't kill me, she thought as she glanced up at Imraan and looked into his eyes. If I am my mother's daughter, then shouldn't I have her strengths as well as her weaknesses? If she has this power, then shouldn't I be able to find it in myself too? Look at me, Imraan. Really look at me. Let go of that guilt, that self-hatred, that confusion. You were still a child when she took control of you, just like I was a child when they took control of me. But because you were always physically stronger than her, it's harder for you to accept that you were a victim too. So look at me and see yourself, see both of us, see both of *them*! Let go, Imraan. Let go.

Maddy could barely see, but she focused as hard as she could, drawing the last of the oxygen in her cells to fuel her concentration. She could feel the Sheikh's strong hands crushing her, but she kept her focus on his eyes, trying to draw on instincts that she told herself she had to have buried in there. If she got the worst of her mother, then surely she had the best of her too.

She could feel her windpipe about to collapse, but then suddenly the Sheikh let go, his eyes clearing up as if a cloud had lifted. He blinked and looked down at her, his face going dark, eyes widening in shock. Then he looked at her mother kneeling behind Maddy, and as Gaurina began to mutter something in Arabic, the Sheikh reached out and grabbed *her* by the throat, roaring in anger as he did it.

"This ends now!" he shouted, pressing so hard Maddy was certain Gaurina wouldn't last more than three seconds.

"No!" came the scream from the shadows, and as Maddy's vision returned in splinters, she caught a flash of Khalifa running across the room, picking up the dagger that Maddy had dropped earlier, and then pushing it into Gaurina's side, cutting upwards as Gaurina screamed in agony.

Then Khalifa drew the dagger out, and in one swift move sliced across her own throat, her eyes going wide and then dimming before she crumpled to the floor.

34

The Sheikh watched his mother die, but he felt nothing. Ya Allah, what is wrong with me, he wondered as he turned his attention back to Gaurina, who was curled on her side, bleeding to death as Maddy stared down at her.

"Look at you two, father and daughter," she whispered, her voice so weak Imraan could barely understand the words. "Our beautiful bloodline, mixed forever. May Allah bless you with many children of your own. Father and daughter."

Imraan stared at Gaurina as she smiled, her eyes narrowing for a moment as if she took some strange delight in those last words, as if those last words were her own way of fighting back, slicing deeper than any knife could.

"You say you don't want to be part of this family? You are. In more ways than you can imagine," Gaurina muttered, that smile still on her face. "Think back, Imraan. When was Maddy born? You do not remember, do you? You do not remember that the girl you thought was your step-sister was actually born nine months after you first spilled your seed inside me. You do not remember. Or do you?"

The Sheikh almost choked as the sickness rose up in him. "No," he muttered. "You are lying. That is impossible. I was too young. It cannot be. Your lies will not twist us into the people you want us to be."

"It is not a question of what we want to be. It is a matter of who we *are*! And you two know who you are! Brother and sister. Father and daughter. Man and woman. King and queen. You are all of it, and you know it." Gaurina laughed, coughing as blood poured from her mouth. "You have already put your seed in her, have you not? So there you go. You have already become who you were destined to be. Our work is complete. Our line will go on, stronger than ever, combined in the most beautiful way. All our genes mixed together."

"You're sick," Maddy muttered, staring down at her dying mother. "Please die. Please die now, or I'll put that knife back into you."

The two of them watched in silence as Gaurina took her last breath, and then they looked at one another.

"No," said the Sheikh. "It was her last attempt at twisting us beyond repair. It cannot be true. Our bodies would have known it. Nothing so unnatural could have occurred. We could not have felt what we felt if what she said were true."

Maddy blinked as she stared at the Sheikh, and Imraan could see the faintest of doubts in her eyes. And then he felt that seed of doubt emerge within him too, and he looked away as the sickness rose up in him again. Could it be true? Or was this her last attempt at manipulating them, the last move of a twisted woman, the legacy of a family defined by depravity.

"But these are the people who gave birth to us," Maddy said slowly, the panic spreading across her face as she touched her naked belly. "Who knows what we're capable of feeling, what we're capable of doing, what we're capable of . . . creating. Oh, God, Imraan, what if I'm pregnant? What if I'm carrying our child? What if—"

She looked at that dagger, covered in the blood of three people. Then she looked at the Sheikh and took a breath.

"No," said Imraan. "Maddy, no. Let us think for a moment. We cannot trust anything that woman says. There are medical DNA tests that will—"

"I don't need any fucking tests to tell me that my

DNA is twisted beyond repair," Maddy snarled. She picked up the dagger and rose to her feet, standing naked before him as the Sheikh straightened and faced her. "We're not going to give these people what they wanted. Our line ends today. All of it."

"Maddy," he said, taking a step closer and then stopping when he saw the look in her eyes. "You are not thinking clearly. Neither of us is thinking clearly. Put the knife down, and let us focus on getting out of here."

"We aren't getting out of here. Neither of us. Stop right there or I'll scream my head off and let those armed men finish it."

"You are not going to kill me," the Sheikh said quietly. But he did stop his advance. "So what is your move?"

Maddy blinked as she looked at the dagger. Then she raised it to her own throat. "The only move left. I can't live with that thought in my head, knowing that what Gaurina said could be true, knowing that my own mother would *want* that to happen!"

"It is not true. Search yourself, Maddy. We could not have felt that attraction for each other if we have common blood between us," said the Sheikh, a part of him sensing that he was trying to convince himself of it too. "I understand the doubt. I understand that we can't trust our genetics, knowing how twisted our parents are. But I also understand that what we've felt over the past week is real, perhaps the only thing real in all this madness."

Maddy shook her head, pressing the edge of the blade until a faint line of blood appeared along her throat. "It doesn't matter. Even if she's lying, to know that she would want us to believe that . . . Imraan, that's even worse, in a way! And that's who we are! The spawn of these people! It's over, Imraan. I'm at the end of my rope here. You're right. I won't kill you. But I'm done. If you get out, good for you. But I'm taking myself out of the picture. I won't be responsible for polluting the earth with our sickness any longer."

The Sheikh glanced at his naked stepsister, her body glistening with perspiration, her breasts hanging heavy, nipples pointing delicately off to either side in perfect symmetry. He glanced shamelessly at her dark triangle, her thick thighs, her muscular calves. He felt his cock move, and right then and there he decided that he was right, his body was right. Gaurina herself had said it earlier, hadn't she? Trust your body. Your body knows the truth.

Yes, the Sheikh thought as he slowly undid the buckle of his belt. He was already shirtless, and as he dropped his trousers and pushed down his underwear, releasing his cock and letting his erection spring out, he saw the way Maddy's nipples stiffened on their own. That is the only way out. That is the only test that will convince her, perhaps convince me.

"What are you doing, you sick bastard?" she muttered, glancing at his cock and then into his eyes even as he saw the way she tightened her buttocks.

"You know what I am doing, he growled, stepping out of his clothes and standing before her fully naked. "If we can't trust our memories, can't trust our parents, can't trust our genetics, then we have to trust the only thing that is left: Our bodies."

"Stand back," she whispered, her hand shaking as she pointed the dagger at him and then held it against her throat again as if she couldn't decide, didn't want to decide. "Imraan, we're sick. We're diseased from the inside out. We have to end our line. You know it."

"Just the desire to end your line because you think you are sick proves that you are *not* sick, does it not?" the Sheikh whispered as he took another step towards her. "It proves you care about the world, about the kind of person you are, about the kind of child you might put into this world. And that means there is hope. It means we can rise above our genetics. Make choices that overrule the choices made for us. There is hope, Maddy. Hope that we can get the ending *we* want, not the ending they wanted!"

He saw her expression change, her knife-hand shake, and the moment of hesitation was enough. With a silent grunt he leapt at her, grabbing her wrist and twisting the knife from her hand. He pressed his other hand over her mouth so she wouldn't scream, and he drove her backwards until she slammed against the red walls of the empty room.

He looked into her eyes long and hard as he felt his cock rise up and line squarely with her warm slit. He could feel her heat, sense her wetness, smell her arousal. His body was right, he knew. So was hers.

"This is the test," he whispered, glancing down at his cock and then into her eyes. "It got us here, and it will take us past this." Slowly he reached down and grasped his own shaft, moving his swollen cockhead against her clit until he felt her body shudder in response. "Yes? Yes, Maddy?"

She blinked once, and he felt her nod as he pressed up against her. And as he massaged the head of his cock into her opening, reaching down with his left hand and raising her thigh, he removed his hand from her mouth and leaned in and kissed her.

It does not matter, came the thought as both his tongue and his cock entered her at the same time. I am now everything and everyone to her. That was the commitment I made when I took her the first time. That is the commitment I will hold on to for the rest of our days. The way our bodies are reacting convinces me that we share no blood, that what we are doing is not unnatural. But in a way it does not matter, because I will be everything to her from now on: friend and family, brother and lover, father and husband.

35

She knew he was right the moment she felt his cock push into her, the moment she tasted his kiss, the moment she felt his strong hands press her ass as he began to drive his hips and pump into her. She was his, and it didn't matter what of his she was: his sister, his lover, his friend, his daughter, or his wife. It didn't fucking matter, because he was all the man she needed, all the man she wanted. He was all her men in one, and although she could tell just by the way her body was opening up for him that there was no way what Gaurina had said was true, she decided it didn't matter. They'd passed the test. And now it was just the two of them, always and forever.

So as their mothers lay dead on the floor, their fathers dead in other places, the two of them kissed like it was a honeymoon, fucked like it was their first time, came like it was the big bang that created the universe.

He took her against the wall, on the floor, from in front and behind. He poured his load deep into her vagina, then twenty minutes later into the far depths of her anus. He held her bleeding throat as she clawed his ravaged back. They were embracing themselves as much as they were embracing each other in that moment, claiming themselves as much as they were claiming each other in their orgasms. It was the only way out, the only way to make sense of it, the only way forward.

And so when they heard the commotion outside the room, the guards shouting in Arabic and then the unmistakable sounds of American voices ordering them to put their guns down, the two children lay naked against each other like Adam and Eve before the Fall, innocent and free, free from guilt, free from shame.

"You must be John Benson," the Sheikh said when the door swung open and a white-haired man stood there. "Tell me, Mister Benson. Was this how you hoped things would end when you made your deal with the devil?"

36

"**I** made the only deal I could at the time," Benson said, looking at Maddy and then the Sheikh. "And sure, over the years I considered taking them out. But I left them alive because I knew that someday the two of you would want answers, answers that had to be experienced first-hand. So I let them live. I kept eyes on them over the years, knowing that the old Sheikh would one day reach out for a last taste of the power he'd enjoyed. And then I did what I do best: Set up the situation and let it play out. It was the right thing to do." He took a breath and smiled. "It was also the smart thing to do, because now I have two allies running the Kingdom of Wahaad, instead of a Sheikh with no memory of his past."

The three of them were on a private plane from Paris to the United States, with Benson sitting across from them. He'd cleaned up the mess in Paris—which was easy, since the old Sheikh and his queens had officially been dead for twenty years anyway.

"Why were you even involved with our parents to begin with?" Maddy asked firmly, feeling Imraan's grip on her hand tighten as she spoke. "Is it true you were trying to recruit my mother?"

Benson narrowed his gaze at her and then slowly turned away, glancing out the window as the clouds slowly moved past. "I'm always recruiting," he said quietly. "Once you two get settled, I'll be in touch. Count on it."

Once we get settled, Maddy thought with a smile as she looked up at Imraan and then past him towards those same lazy clouds. Will any of this ever settle? Will we ever leave behind the legacy of our parents, the design of our genes?

Perhaps that isn't our destiny, came the thought as she considered what Benson had said with that enigmatic smile. Perhaps there is a strange dance between genetics and destiny, free will and fate. Maybe we get to choose which parts of our parents we carry with us and which parts we leave behind. Perhaps that is the next test we're going to face. Perhaps it's a test that we'll be facing every day for the rest of our lives.

But you know what, she thought as the Sheikh looked down at her like he could understand what she was thinking, like he was the only one who could understand: there's no one I'd rather face that test with than you. My man. My *every* man: father and husband, brother and lover, friend and family. Always and forever.

Always and forever.

∞

EPILOGUE
SIX MONTHS LATER

Maddy touched her pregnant belly and looked up at the Sheikh. "What if . . ." she said quietly, even though she didn't believe it for a moment.

The Sheikh grunted. "We can always run DNA tests. Or we can just ask Benson."

Maddy sighed. "Do you think it's troubling that we didn't ask Benson anything about them?"

"Do you think he would have answered?"

Maddy shrugged. "That's not the point. We didn't even ask. We didn't ask if what we know about who our real parents are is true, if *any* of what happened is true."

The Sheikh reached around her ample waist and pulled her close. They were in that same outdoor verandah, watching that desert spring bubble up from the earth as the sun set over the golden dunes of the Wahaadi desert.

"We did not ask, because we do not care. We have chosen to ignore genetics. We have chosen to write our own destiny. We have chosen to be free of the past."

"But can we? What if our unborn child is a deformed monster?"

The Sheikh shrugged, gesturing towards that pool formed by the desert spring. "Then we will drown the bastard and try again, my love," he said with a completely straight face.

Maddy screamed in mock horror, punching the Sheikh on the chest so hard he roared in pain. "You sick asshole! How can you even—"

"Or perhaps I will just drown you for hitting me so hard, you twisted creature," the Sheikh grunted, rubbing his chest where there would almost certainly be a bruise in a few hours. "That will end it, yes? Just the way you wanted."

Maddy laughed as she involuntarily ran her finger along the thin scar she'd made when she almost cut her own throat. She understood why they hadn't asked Benson any questions, why they hadn't run any DNA tests. Yes, part of it was because she did trust in what her body was telling her, what his body was telling him. But part of it was also because of what that sliver of doubt was doing to her, to them both, to their relationship. How that tiny bit of "what if" added a hint of darkness to their lives . . . lives that were now full of light and hope.

Because they were born of darkness, and although they had chosen the light, decided to write their own future together, they understood that it was the darkness that made the light seem so bright.

And so they would carry that last bit of it with them in the form of that "what if," letting it create that subversive energy, the energy of opposites.

That same energy that gives the earth its spin . . .

The same energy that gives love its luster . . .

The same energy that makes the twists of a story as much fun as its ending.

∞

FROM ANNABELLE WINTERS

Thanks for reading.

Join my private list at **annabellewinters.com/join** to get steamy epilogues, exclusive scenes with side characters, and a chance to join my advance review team.

And do write to me at **mail@annabellewinters.com** anytime. I really like hearing from you.

Love,
Anna.

Printed in Dunstable, United Kingdom